GRACE

In the Concordia Library,

This book to a great
institution!

John Dean
13 October 2002

GRACE

BY JOHN BARR

AN EPIC POEM

STORY LINE PRESS
1999

Published by Story Line Press, Three Oaks Farm, PO Box 1240, Ashland, OR 97520-0055
www.storylinepress.com

This publication was made possible thanks in part to the generous support of the Nicholas
Roerich Museum, the Andrew W. Mellon Foundation, the National Endowment for the
Arts, and our individual contributors.

Book design by Lysa McDowell
Cover Acrylic Painting, "India: Long Night's Journey" © Betty Laduke
Text lithographs © Betty Laduke

Library of Congress Cataloging-in-Publication Data Pending

Barr, John, 1943–
    Grace : an epic poem / by John Barr
        p.   cm.
    ISBN 1-885266-85-5 (cloth : alk. paper)
    ISBN 1-885266-81-2 (pbk. : alk. paper)
    I. Title
PS3552.A731837G7   1999
811'.54—dc21   99-41978
                                                CIP

For Penny, who perish the thought.

A NOTE ON THE AUTHOR

The poems of John Barr, President Emeritus of the Poetry Society of America, have been published in four books over the past decade: *The War Zone, Natural Wonders, The Dial Painters* and *The Hundred Fathom Curve.* He also serves on the boards of Yaddo and Bennington College, the latter as Chairman. He is a businessman and lives with his family in Westchester County, New York. But he is merely amanuensis. The real author of this book is a Caribbean gardener named Ibn Opcit. Opcit was first heard talking in 1988 and was last seen, still talking, in a Soviet spacecraft circling the earth.

A NOTE ON THE LANGUAGE

The voices in *Grace* use the freedoms of a Caribbean-like speech to get away with murder. Elizabethan English—Shakespeare's English—felt free to coin words, to discard the Latinate baggage of prefix and suffix when it got in the way, cheerfully to impress a noun into service as a verb, and to choose sense over syntax, always, should a choice be required. So with this invented dialect, which seeks the energy and economy of dialects in general. As that lovely man Anthony Burgess said, "Black English has the right idea."

CONTENTS

THE OVERRUTH HEARINGS

*O*UT. *O*UT. *O*UT.

"Oyez. Oyez.

Now is this Court of the Carib Kingdom of Grace in motion.
His Extreme Unction, the Punch Press of our Penal Code,
the Dependable Jack Hammer of our Jurisprudence,
the Significant Shareholder of our Commonwealth,
the avid golfer, the urbane and stunningly fair
Daniel O'Boi Arap judgmenting. All rise."

"Down. The case of *This Place v. Daniel Overruth.*
Call the first lyre."

"State your name. Name your State."

"Ibn Opcit, your Worship, of de State of Grace."

"Tell his Almightiness the basis for you here
tryin' his impatience. In your own words, tell."

"I de gardener. I keeper de covenant
of de elements wid de Overruth estate.
When de sun busy elsewhere, when de rain miss,
I make up de difference.
Little potash, little phosphor, lime,
I keep de grounds shy of exhaustion.
I do de wormwork wid de pitcherfork,
work in peat, give de humus lungs.
I spread de good news of de compost heap.
I help de heartflops tooth on nitrogen,
de fescue green and deepen, de beds of purple fidget
swell like dey was pregnant..."

"Get to de point."

"Last week, de afternoon, I finish cuttin'
de doppleganger and hullabaloo, de laurellie
and ballyhoo for de crystal arrangements inside.
I standin' by de window, de big house, waterin'
when dis gentlemun arrive. He been here before.
A long drink-o-water name of Flavian Wyoming,
he encounter de Mistress Hepatica Overruth within.
(She spend days on her hair. She just finish a spacial.)

Now de lady, she love de silver lewd.
It be her point of approach. The gentleman, he know this.
He know her kiss leave *marks*. He know
she a ballbuster of de first magnitude.
No time for 'Boy!', he treat her like a sudden rug.
Into the bedoir he play Simon Segue.
No frill, no twine, he delectate de lady.
Like he were makin' up a smoke or lickin'
de scupper clean, he doin' grace notes wid his tongue.
He a trencherman to admire. De lady, she pleased
to be his aspic meal, his piece of thunder pie.
She holler 'Mon éclair! You One-Shot Kangaroo!'
De gentleman, he produce his próduce
like a corporate salami, and she hers,
like a surgery scar still angry red wid healing.
Den he settle his equipment in de lady's outback
an' he spud de well. And while his tool down-hole,
I hear de car door slam. And just when he find de pay zone,
just when he givin' her de salt shot, in walk
de Marquand Flactree de Monback O'Boi Overruth himself.
Quicker dan a seven-headed goat snatcher
de Marquand have dat cockpud on his back.
And de Marquand, he produce *his* próduce,
out of his cane a quite whippy sword.
And like a 'blue' on de fantail, going home—
*spray of scales, fling of guts, two deep strokes,
the oily meat is yours*—he filet dat man."

"Dis witness available for de cross."

"Ibn Whatnot. Dat be your name?"

"Opcit be de name, your Onlyness."

"Whatnot, tell how you come to be here
botherin' his Gruffness today."

"I walkin' down D'arcy this a.m.,
eatin' cracklepone an' a rum touche.
Takin' de single air, I reach dat place
where de low road cleave de hill and,
half and half, de shoulders marl and show
de macaroni life laid down forevermore.
I see de squad car where it squat to feed
wid its ready radar on de flow of speed.
Dis day, man say 'Ibn, come here.'"

"Dey use force?"

                    "No, he semblable.
Say 'Been a killin'. Somebody got to say.'"

"Whatnot, you a poet, is you not?"

"   "

"Say up. De Court can't hear."

"I quill a bit."
                    "A bit? Why, Whatnot,
some folks say you writin' all de *time*.
Now, Ibn, be you printin' some of these?"

"No, sir."

                    "Why, Ibn, I believe dat's wrong.
We find dat you been printin' dese yere poetries

over the name of Daniel Ownyore.
Why you hide behind another name?
Sound to me somewhat precarious."

"   "

"May it please your Steely Intellect, I'll read
de followin', found in dis man's place of privacy."

O_2O_2

Iron, he is steel, he good for the auto hood,
resisting crumple when the eye averted from the car ahead,
but iron, like a dog always ready to run off,
want to change and particle to rust. He yearn to be ore.

Copper no better. Try as he might he can't hold
that salmon shine. Athwart the salad air,
lichen and liverspot, he go green.
Except for Ibn's elbow grease and his dissuadin' Brasso,
copper nothin' but a throatful of oxide.

De world so full of lively elements.
Him water wear and roll, till de stream bed's
boulders nothin' but a bed of robin's eggs.
Him water get a grip in a nevermind of gneiss—
the tiniest fissure—and watch him freeze and fracture
granite like a mouse skull in a owl's claw.

Air, don't mention it. Little methane, little argon,
and ozone—oh yes, O_3, dat necessary radical.
But in de midst of all dem jump-down, spin-around

heptagonals come de ransacker name of O_2,
de Great White lookin' for de big score.
O_2: spider lover of metals.
O_2: procuress for fire.
O_2: de hunger in Quine d'Rodéo's lungs.

"Now *dat* be a jolly artifact we all damn better worry about.
Opcit, be you talkin' here 'bout nothin' less
than the deterioration, the decline,
the downfall, destruction and demise of this yere State of Grace?
Your Severity, dis man appear to have anarchy on his mind.
But dat is not de most of my concern.
Opcit, you a womanizer?"

"Sir?"

"Well, you lovin' so much de *ground,* de *sun,*
de floral events around de Overruth estate,
I wonder if you be a lover of de quim as well.
Your Rectitude, it would offend the Court to hear
the most of this man's love yammer, but please the Court
I'll read one more from dis man's ark of privacy:

DE BLACK WID DE WRONG-COLORED EYES

2 a.m., de stars burn wid de might of daylight
and de black wid de wrong-colored eyes is walkin' home.
Home from Bald Mountain where he ride de night away
above gentle divide an' downy defile.
Home from de cave of winds
where he chat de fickly spirit up,
he homage de tiny puckernut.

No sittin' home to choke the chicken, he,
dis charter member of de charmed sperm club
tame de weirding room itself, de egress of gods.
No aging ecstat of de hot slot, he,
dis master of de troubled clef, de doubled cleft
make of last week's "Oh, no," tonight's "Oh, ho."

He abracadabra de pelvic tell.
"Dugway darlin', he say. "Pellucid beauty."
Den how dey bower and dey devour
de fruit dat is not consumed—
de primates' breadfruit—knockers and nuts.
He proffer de wrinkled ogive. She dress de lingam.
He raise his flag on gunboat thighs
dat have no sovereign interest to protect.
His consid'rable piston she cylinder.
Here in Grace prosperity run out to eke.
But de lacunar moon, de cislunar satellites
party like Mardi Gras,
and de blue-eyed black is gettin' home at 2 a.m.

"Now, Opcit, you testify dat you was waterin' de fidget beds
next de big house when dis incident occurred.
What was de implement you use to deliver the water?"

"De garden hose."

"So you were standin' at de window, lookin' in,
wid de hose in your hand. Now Ibn Opcit or Ibn Whatnot
or Daniel Ownyore, tell de Court, was de hose
you holdin' in your hand a garden hose
or was it your black natural own?"

"Say what?"

"Your Indignity, I suggestin' dis man have
de mind for anarchy and poontang, and dat in fact
he appear to be a crack fiend wid voyeuristic tendencies.
Ibn Opcit, do you abjure this unseemly testament?"

"Do not."

"Your Divine Excrescence, dis witness witless.
He a dipstick wid no show of oil."

"Let the witness have a care. You are what you say you saw."

"Your Honorbright, this no flimsy pew.
I saw what I say. I say what I saw. I swear a great oath."

"Your 'Rascibility, dis kaffir a stupid jongleur.
Dis lyre a liar. Opcit, do you recant?"

"Can't."

"Then I invoke the German jeopardy."

"German jeopardy has been provoked.
Does the witness understand that he
may be responsible for what he see?"

"Wait!"

"No good! Too late!"

"Of this Edwardian rowf towf, enough.
Ibn Opcit, under the laws of the State of Grace,

you are found guilty of what you see. The Court is choiceless.
The hammer of our indignation has been tripped
and you shall pay the painful pittance,
the full farthing of the arrested utopia.
A month of Sundays you will marinate in jail.
Then from the flagpole of our Capitol
a significant piece of you shall witness
the price this act from the rest of you exacts:
Iron to O, stone to bone, hemp hung.
Take this one away."

                        "All rise.
Now is Justice" — *Out. Out. Out.* — "done."

THE
ECLOGUES
OF
OPCIT

I. Genesises

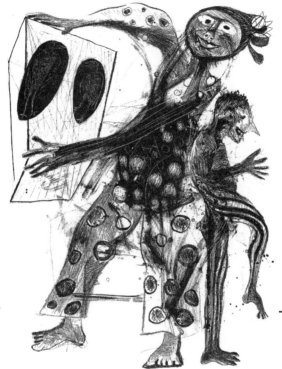

Things unseen count coup on you. The ant, wid its nose
for necrosis, try Ibn's toe, Ibn's ear, then turn away.
The mosquitoess, who bring me a bracelet of bites,
a ring of harm, find wid de radars in her feet.
Surviving yet another of her approaches in the dark,
she grapple, gravid, wid what it is to be Opcit:
wid hairline legs grasp the braces of his body hair;
wid friendly razor stir the pot of Ibn's ichor.
De rats dey disembark at night all appetite.

Dere's a fair amount of controversy as to who
who on de feedin' chain. Uppermost I know *we* is not.
We appear to be somewhere midway between
de flea bane and de rat supply.
As to fat and carbohydrate, Geode, we out of de running,
we down to a gristly overture for protein.

   We in a Waste Not Want Not mode, Geode;
dis place a weight-watcher's paradise.
In de arms of scurvy we watch ourselves at both ends
expurgate, watch our avoirdupois decline.
Not much to do, we loosen de latch, see what de bowels make
of hazy, see-through rations: Dere go de Sapper salad,
de Limpet stew. Dere go de Bangalore salami.
We get urine's contained metaphor—white dat's yellow—
we get a burley stew, a possible flush.
On de subject of bowels, connoisseurs, we develop
an intellectual capital structure. Dis place
have limited opportunities for getting into trouble.

   To the Creationists' colony I say "Horse Nanny."
I hear dere man, one of de heads of his age,
speakin' his mind wid a piece of chalk.
A Professor of Ecstatics from Cryogenic State,
he say "De world de work of a Raswickian demiurge.
He a mort fellow and live on a planetary diet.
Like a Tovidian Rock Jock he say,
Now we gonna move some heaven,
and now we gonna move some earth.
As a man hawk a spittle for de far side
he dispose of his guests in great spheres,
dey drift off like voice balloons in Batman.

One such, wid bedraggled human cargo,
he send off in a dirge of likening."
And dis dere iddy biddy history of Earth.
I hear him, wearin' de short pants of achievement,
launch—just like dat—one bad idea after another.
As he reach ever higher orders of mistake
I feel the cold dingle of ice applied to a man's spare parts.

I raise my hand. "Yes," he say, "are we in search
of something to disagree about?" "Maybe dis all
elaborate preamble for something I don't understand,"
I say, "but dis like a paper bag dat can't
hold itself together in de rain."
He suck de rattly straw of his pipe.
"You are asking what, precisely, of whom?"
"You make of de world a autoplexy turnbuckle. Fair Enough.
Dat you support wid de Moreover and de Furthermore.
I can see de Monkey-see Monkey-do of dat.
But *den* you make a pronounciation of our end—
and you support it wid a hatful of natural history.
Now *dat* create hedonic damages. Dis
de consequential Bolivar we lookin' at."
"Nothing pymlical nor physiolical about it.
Let me, by extrapolation of artifice, explain:
Dese are things to think about in a distracted way...
Dere's more here dan we can handle in a single logjam...
These are lower-tier tumultuai...
Let's fit dem into some truisms we can understand..."
(He not too meticulous on any of dis;
he into the soupçon method of appliqué.) I say,
"All dis as random as matching buttons to holes
when Ibn dress in de morning in de dark." "Ah,"

he say, "we come to the Lesser Antilles of the argument."
In a riddance, a log phlegm of dour daum,
he assert dismissive ambiguity.
He refer me to the Cantabrigian Overlect.
"Your use of de Oddswaddian Circumspect," I say,
"might throw a man of lesser scent.
But just as a hog can't smell its own jasper
and de fragrance of dog gavotte is close to extreme
for all but its owner, you walkin' in dog scrumption
but think you are scentless in dis affair."
"And *your* use of the deformed abrivative
is definitionally inconstant."
"In a Silesian context dat *might* be true, but if you going
to reify as in, 'Reigate Demartia,'
dat would be an Encyclical O'Schwartz."
"You going to test me on the difference?"
"Dat would be putting to sea in a part time boat. "
He stand there, his red face pingled with punks:
"Tell me this. Which of us is the Doctor
of Forensic and Surroundative Medicine?"
"To live in de reflected light of a bad idea,"
I say, "is to move in a misshapen orderliness.
Your theory be like a badly-flawed pregnancy."
"And *you* have a head like a shredded coconut.
Who are *you*," he say," to be beneath contempt?"
"But why," say I, "am I being *peremptoried?*"
"*What* are you," he say, "the signpost to Damascus?
And which of us is the *Visiting* Professor of Italics?"
He stand there waiting for the next enlargement.
I ask him to open dis to full investigation
so we may know de authors of dis crapplestance
and circumlong. "That's like trying to get to know
somebody at a orgy. That's not why we're here.

We need a construct to put these people in their *place*.
We don't need the indelicate response of oafs.
And you don't need to understand it, you just need
to embrace the consensual regalia.
You just need to stand in a line and compromise.
But fickle is as fickle does, m'lad, and talking to you
is like trying to embrace an armful of canaries.
As you pursue the trackless wastes of whatever's on your mind,
just remember, we talkin' about microns of dusty abstruse.
What we got here is a torrent of self-inflicted flux."
"What we got here," I mutter, "is a six- or seven-
thousand yard penalty. What we got here
is de maximal deflagonhotte."

Although I take both sides of dis ontology—
and regularly lose—I don't descend into all dat pudmire.
I favor another overture to de Overall.
(Some of dis I had from a text on Cuban science,
de rest of it Opcitical.) I favor de view
dat lively elements—sun, wind, rain—
folding and folding in a Melchior surmise
cause a catch in de fabric of de firmament,
a purple twinge. As guildsmen blow a phlegm of molten glass
into a party-colored Whatnot—with secondaries,
with sugary incendiaries dat cause dem to stand back and say
"Dat's a big fuckin' fire. Dat's de trouble with being real."—
dey make of a No-Where a Now-Here.
As long as it takes to know what you think,
it cool like a simmery, bilious recollection,
it become a load-bearing member of the universe.
Dey set it, still groggy with light, spinning on its polarities
so the days are eaten by nights are eaten by days....
De seas distil like a salt sweat after labor.

De world wear a watery epiderm
which dey robe wid sacerdotal sand.
For quite some time de world abide a hunger for green
until de feeling was dat dis could have been done better.
But den de wind dey bring forth from dere treasuries,
a cool front tease an allotment of rain out of de upper fissures,
de rivers belly by de low roads for de sea,
de earth unfurl its foremost flag.

      Of the Americas they set the South to the east of the North.
And east of everywhere, an oceanic bank
make of a Cambrian reef a chowder of life:
plenty of bivalve with the duodenal mouth;
brain coral and such, dat imitate geometry;
wrasse and angelfish, rays and morays.
Careful of upheaval, dis edge of earth
shove above de oceanic verge.
Pretty soon — couple of million years —
it green up (something always come to make a meal):
conifer attempts, a forest of approaches
to *tannenbaum*. And den Walt Whitman's live oak,
cognomen of chlorophyll, make a stand.
Butterflies, more colorful close to the equator,
dine on mud, fruit, animal sweat.
De spider move his needles in de greatness of his kind.
Lord of its bush, a tanager
lay down the law in colors and call.
In all but name we have de state of Grace.

      Dat leave de moon and our relationship to it.
Everything else in the heavens is a point or circle,
only de moon show us an out-of-round — a waxed or waned.
De *new:* like a bent man bowed to hoist a stone of earthshine.

Finest of night fruit, de casing moon, a rind around a sweetmeat.
De *gibbous:* demimondal, swollen like de unhalf of your heart.
De *full:* high noon, high feeding time
for things wid platter eyes or none.
It's de blue crew subbing for de gold!
Raccoons army march from drains,
skunks devour de food of sleeping pets,
de field mouse wid geometric progeny
answer de hunting prowess of de owl.
Or *waned:* a depleted ball, from de right side disappearing,
its tail tucked under like a lobster on de boil.

Everything else in the heavens is a single color.
Only de moon across de book of hours harps a chord.
When it rise in de bolt hole, low and complete,
de moon wear colors of menace—umber, hamburg—
so swarthy you wait for it to turn for de profile shot.
Out of de quell of dat Sicilian regard it rise
through tones of derby, bat, chalcedony
to a psalm of harvest—honey, apricot, wheat—
where it be more cheddar, better at being a sphere.
It reach de age of metals. A bight of bronze; early iron;
edge of adze; equipment grips wid de paint worn off.
Through varieties of silver it chromatize—
café au lait, cognac, linen, peregrine—
to de heavy end: Palladium, osmium, californium.

It zenith: A day of its own, electrostatic blue!
(You see last night how it clean and block de cell?)
But having done its best, now the moon do less.
The moon of 3 a pharmacological moon:
arsenic, camphor, ash, blister, corpse.
Of 5, forensic: a fern-perfect fossil of itself.

By 6 de moon burn off de last of its reserves;
de washed-up hulk pay up, haul off.

    Den de first bird dispatch de peaceable dark wid "Oleo. Oleo."
Pretty soon birds be jackin' off all over de woods,
dey appear to be considerin' riot. Den de wind
of de corn make rows of constant motion.
The wagon of Ollie Tricknorth under agricultural load
creak by, de first man-motion of de day.
De sun rise in de bolt hole, low and complete.

    De moon be here to teach us de beauty of change.
De moon be here to teach us de beauty of return.

II. I Been to New York. Once.

Aمerica? It's a carve of a continent,
a land so vast, between de surge eternal
and de surge eternal, de clocks cannot agree.
Where gathers of basalt de size of mountain chains
and plains de size of serious seas—whole flats of a map—
cause us to say, *Here was a gravity estoppel.*
(Imagine a turmoil of topography

where a couple of crustal plates really went at it:
One hit de other a glancing subduction, de other
answer wid a roundhouse 6.7 on de Richter.)
Imagine a land before de borders are etched: De blue fumble
of de mountains of de Nevada Dissimular
keep their distance, hold their snow like a gathered skirt.
They do with the late sun what they will, lay claim,
with a kind of oracular *Oh See*, to be a region.
Out of dere extreme exotics, rivers find
by a sidelong slide to gravity the flat lands—
basins of black soil, the long reach of fields
toward alfalfa, toward the brushed hair of oats—
where columbiads of cottonwood follow
the deep reversals of their getting there.
Big dams are little in the hoot and holler
of the valleys of the North where blown mist,
sideways rain give rise to greves of Englemann spruce,
where glaciers in Spring fail like riverine
patti-melts under skies cause us to say
Here is an afford of possibility.
Under the eraserless sun of the South,
in a clamor of heat dat pass for India,
hurricanes clear like one more grimpen bombast,
and swamp gas gather in hollows ready for the match.
One of the world's richest biotas, cause us to say
This place miss its dinosaurs.
This land still working on becoming coal.

De country laid out in Bakelite strips,
edged with Gas to Go, Motels to Stay.
Off road, de countryside retain with difficulty
its capacity to glitter after rain.

From sticky pantoons and outland flats
rise Dallas like a glass salute, rise
Chicago like a seat of phosphorescent dreams,
rise towns with names like lamentations.
Omaha with its defrequented stockyards,
Oshkosh imprinted with alleys, Kenosha with sad swept streets
cause us to read "Minnesota Town Requests Right to Die."
A land where factories de size of Michigan discover
over and over dat humans don't make good machines.
Cause us to say, *Here was a destiny made manifest.*
People of de Southwest reduce to squeezed-down expectations.
Southern folk stay mad. Midwestern folk, knowing dere place
an acquired taste, strive to love the dirt between dere toes.
(All along de border farms in Iowa
we hear dem mutter, *We half in Illinois.*)
People of the Northwest I am told
do not exist and California live in Japan.

    America? A country bathed in the trade winds
of humanity at its most. Huge in the feeding,
in the grip of its sensation hugely impatient,
on to the next—WOP—thing in a *was* of doing.
A country of Whoops and Waitaminute
where no one take time to find good footing
and the ambulances all spell backwards.
Land of diseases dat do not communicate
but dere will be an extra season of contagion
for living in zones of improbability.
A land wid no expertise of poisons in dere culture
but road kills are always acceptable.
A country of impacted traffic where toll collectors,
before they take their station, take a leak.

Cars emerge from oily berms, forge forward
in the holy hope that green will find its light.
Patrol cars pursue dem wid a glitter haste.
Troopers standing in the rain write tickets
out of certain deeply-held beliefs.
Dey are trained in de arts of violent response.
A motorcycle triad idles by
potato potato potato
on a mix of leaned gas, missed opportunities.
Angels from Hell, dey are looking for
the dark crumbling overhangs of de Palisades
where dey will splash messages of love,
their particular hatreds and de year.

America? Home of Costa Rica Étan,
whose arms be garnished wid tatoos, whose bodyguards
all had their throats cut at least once.
As a young man starting out, throwing acid, he find
about himself he cast a radius of fear.
Étan determine to make his career in the business of fear:
its inspiration, cultivation, management.
On de kind of sullen anger dat blow up powder trains
he ride the creative curves of imbalance
down to the sinister bands of holding,
to the middle of macabre. He specialize in de law laid low:
Retailing ardent spirits; White slaving
("We hear some of you girls been faking climaxes.
Not to mention all the laughing in the bathroom.").
"What I can't stand," Étan say, "is the ineffectually crooked."
Trails of human debris he leave behind,
who cut his partner's throat with "I just change de rules,"
who send his enemies to the sinter barn
which place resemble an inefficient butcher shop,

where feedback is close to immediate.
(His bullet, delivered of a small-bore pistol,
was directed wid care and concern. It give de Convulser's heart
something to work on. It work, but it can't spit up
de metal pebble, it find itself in full paroxysm.
His aorta he embrace as he embrace his fate.
Again Étan give him a remembrancer, right between
de eyes. A man wid holes, he revert
to de waxen state, a tinkering machine at rest.)
From all dis his lawyers—compellers and restrainers,
de longshoremen of dere society—
hold him harmless, wid not a flitch of consequence.
But when Étan suggest, ever so mildly, dat perhaps
we have enough books published on de Holycost,
he was padlocked like a hasp seated in its slug of brass,
he was transported to the Bournemouth Ossiary.
He was taken before de warden, who sit at his desk
like an avalanche, like a man pretending to be a storefront.
An enormous man, wid dumplings for dimples, continually
his belly test the scrimmage line of his belt.
Known to his parents as Encarpio Monpud and to his classmates
as Abe Disjointme, to intimates de Warden was known as
Phlegm Damhammit, and to inmates as the Huron Hard-On.
"Hot day" he say. "It gonna be a hot abide.
We sittin' here at de edge of sweat.
So hot, I swear I'm sweatin' out of my gums."
He sip from a cup dat smoke like liquid nitrogen;
wid its jacket of humidity, something he not going to share.
"You been mirandized?" he say.
And he read him de By Whom and For What Reason.
A large man used to picking up things wid one hand,
he invite Étan to partake of de informality of his extreme.

Étan sit down hard, right on de scrabbly assize.
"Dis your Exit Interview," de Warden say.
"Dis the 10 o'clock before the 3 o'clock
when you are truly out of *papier toilette.*
Just hours shy of the Devil's damn,
this the Bend-Over-and-Kiss-a-You-Ass Good-By.
So give me your deep attention.
Perhaps there's a standard of intrinsic worth
but what is doable is done, what is done takes undoing.
Some of your crimes are uckier than others:
causing gridlock on a shopping day;
predatory behavior at de airline counter
(where line jumping, like claim jumping, is an act
often rewarded with a bullet).
And good taste, it seem, is not what you say but who you say it to.
You been weighed and found wanton. You got tendencies.
Like a shit head on a mufflerless motorcycle
you ride on your own obnoxious próduce. To me,
you as guilty as a pile of dog gavotte in de living room."
Étan reply, "De left half of my brain been acting up again.
I have what you could call a rich interior life.
I live to de standards of my age,
I take de most careful aim possible.
But every year, it seems, it takes more education,
more work, more luck to succeed dishonestly."
Étan speak of the seem and the unseem, the provocatives,
the prospect of the body drop, the need to find
new ways to stay alive, to continue conspiracy
"within the standhopes of what I try."
He call for a return to profligacy.
He make a nugatory speech, in which we see
the smoothness of a train serving its multitudes.

De Warden say, "I could just tell by looking:
you like my coffee pot, full of volcanic sounds.
You sit there like a monkey in a bowl of ice.
Well, we in the business of wiping smiles off faces.
You come here, holier than atrophy, dressed
in a larcenous foulard. You sit there in a stoned silence.
To our interlocutors you say *Good Morning*.
Den you give dem de Bronx cheer. You say, *Gimme a slate
of hungry fodder.* Well here's de paillard to dat refrain.
Here we gather to a different set of rigors.
People stand in line to throw up here. We watch dem,
like bars of soap, visibly depleting by the day.
We think of the body as a rack on which to hang
a suit; we have our inmates professionally dry cleaned.
We think of the body as a weather vane in a hurricane.
Think of the melon skull atop the neck stalk.
Think of the crucible skull (therein the *rinse* of brains)
atop the supportive spine so prone to dislocation.
Think of the eating hole and the breathing hole sharing
the same cave, so prone to the surprise of asphyxiation.
Think of the hand, the manipulative five.
Think of the fingers, soft palps of overreach:
ten random acts, ten opportunities to do better.
Think of the demispheres of the 'gluts,
met above the uneasy exit with its slick of shit.
In the time it take to say, you go from *Good Morning*
to a mumble of miserichord.
You just have to tell us when enough is too much
and we will make a miniseries of your pain."
One thing about Étan, he don't ride de rear
of de deference bus. He say, *I say joss to dat.*
Wid barely disguised animalistic glee de Warden say,

"When a dog dies de universe is smaller by a German pup,
but you gonna be smoked history and de universe
will be not one wit less. You'll be famous for being dead
and dat's de blister truth." Étan give a binary blink:
"I been busy but I been good. I don't litter. I save de empties..."
"Dis not so difficult as trigonometry," de Warden say.
"Let me talk to you in a language you can understand.
We gonna spare you the stress of an unmade bed.
We gonna manifest your destiny.
We gonna show your head in an exploded view.
If dere's an afterlife you'll become acquainted wid heat."
Étan say, "I got nothing to hide. Or if not nothing not much.
Let me try," he say, "to be an honest witness."
He discuss exchanging the right amount of information.
"Names?" de Warden say. "We got names.
Izwattel Herdunsey. Phillip Ointsment. Plenty of names.
Bavartée Conciliachoise. PoleSwitchie Oduberwa.
We got no lack of names. Every while in the once,
somebody does what they're supposed to and gives me pause.
But you don't look like a man acting under the influence of innocence.
More like a cheap suit that can't unremember its wrinkles.
But the dark is an absence that holds. Bear wid me while I
foreshorten time. We going to have you altered.
By diverting all de kilowatts from de city of Kaukauna
we going to create an electric enjambment in your head.
Dere will be an *Oh my Gosh* of pain. You'll have
a Connecticut brainstorm, a high altitude electric fit.
Your head will be redone in repoussé.
Your grasp and grip on chaos will be impossible to behold.
Yours will be a most cerebral hemorrhage,
wid a crack and a *pung*, a flash photolysis.
Your muscles will seize like a bloc of desperated grief.

A sudden ingestion of death-related flux
will cause you to swell in perpetuity.
With a algorithm for a head and your body
an apostrophe, you will die in place."
Étan betray a trickly sparkle, a cravat of sweat.
He tug a meretricious forelock. *Sensei*, he say, *Gimme a break.*
"Now don't," de Warden say, "you be an inept bodiddly.
Don't, like an inexpensive wine, you throw a sediment.
De man will be here minutely. By all means take advantage
of our penitentiary kitchens for a last engendered meal.
(Once we had a Irish hunger faster here
(a Abyssinian Irishman of no account):
He refuse all nourishment except Bombay
gin martinis wid a splash of bitters and a twist.)
The chef does well with the Chicken and Shrimp Synapse;
and if your stomach going to take the rest of the day off
I recommend you end with the Apricot Condign."
Étan, returned, avail himself of a balanced meal:
Glucose, fructose, dectose, mactose (but he hold on de salsa).
He start with Eggs Urbanico, a Hoffnagel waffle,
and a scuttle of marmalade. Dis he follow wid a Marconi salad
(dot dot dot, dash dash dash, dot dot dot).
He eat his fill, whole bayous, of okra and etcetera.
He quaff drafts of deflected brew, empaled ale.
He end with Elba fudge, a *gringo* of cheese,
and an apple "with its sometime, certain sweet."
The leftovers he send to the Warden's den.
And now, in bombard overalls and cropped head,
down cellblocks of defeated air the Last Mile he begin.
"Dearly Beloved-a, foregive-a dem all
dere cheesy linguine and base-a-ball."
Past cells of the sniffers and the lickers and the

experimenters in bathrooms, feasting in the dark.
"Death by Knockout, man. Death by Knockout."
"Go manifest your destiny."
"See you on the other side of Hell."
Hit wid a clinging fear Costa Rica
go off-system in a blank response.
He up and call *Time Out.*
He say *Wait a minute* to de entire affair.
He make a manacled inveigh. He do a yowly gargle.
He make a medley of bathroom sounds, a complete panoply.
He talk a spectrum of spittle. He use shipyard pejoratives.
He blubber *Bejeezus, man. Gimme a fuckin' break.*
Dey carry him, underpants escutcheoned wid fear;
dey make him sit in a chair like a 3-way plug.
Dutifully dey wait for his last words.
"What the world needs is a better slipknot. Wait.
The women here iron their hair. Wait."
At the summit of his life Costa Rica say
"I need more time to think." And he go
D - D - Dz - z - zz. Dt - Dt - Dzzzzz.

America, where people spend hours a day turning knack into mastery,
where spray paint vandals have de gift of a cloud
but high school cheerleaders never get it right:

         Gimme a Y
         Gimme a P
         Gimme a F A C

America, a country that wear its pockets high,
where whole villages have no body odor
because de people evolve wid enjambed armpits.
A land where player comfort is quite important
but Hank Sledge, star of de Janissary Hoops,
was suspended when a routine analysis found

his specimen to contain heavy concentrations of urine.
(A small race of black giants pummels the air,
poofs the ball through iron hoops in celebration
of reach. Fans in oneness *Moof Moof Moof.*
They gladiator the exits. Accommodation
becomes white noise, becomes Control and What Lets Go.)

Home to Yobubba Behemoth, né Mal Dwoppit,
who change his name to Memorial Bide-a-Wee,
then fine tune that to Marmoreal Monpud,
then legally chuck the whole thing for Yobubba.
Born to a skinny upper stalk, always he feel
a jablonsky of despair dat his was not
de *After* but de *Before Before Before.*
Not for him to walk wid a mincing gait
and go by de name of Imperturb.
Widout apologies to loved ones he move to L.A.
He take a job as a mechanical advantage:
in Valet Parking, the cars he park by pushing.
Wid freaks and gawks, cross-eyed wid strain he push
a car-equivalent to the moon and back.
He reformulate his body wid chemicals.
He emerge from the World Gym in sirloin magnificence.
Misshapen wid muscle, he resemble a musculature
widout de skin. His biceps cable wid strain,
his upper body a single flex as he chin — one-handed — up.
His lower, dat land of big muscles, he work into awestruck legs.
Washboard belly basted wid steroids,
fulcrumed to de point of centroid,
wid incredible clasping power — by the *Teuton* —
he resemble a man in a lobster suit. A riveting narcissist,
of his stance, his strut, self-conscious to a fault.
What was jerked, pressed, laboriously composed of *oof*

now effortlessly performs in mineral oil
before de torso-philes and torso-holics.
He place wid a "Ne Plus Ultra" in the Lats Division
of the Mr. Show. To interviewers he respond
wid a hearty affirmation of *uh-huh*.
He keep a pelvic dossier on his favorite women.
He expect dem to stand in line for his genes.
A bloat of hard, he an Ausable Kick-in-de-Face,
a walking tit for tat, wid a punch to send a man
if need be sprawling into Woebegone.
Yobubba walk in de welter of his weight,
ready for the thickly-muscled Peruvian
man-slammer who will never come.

America, where everybody organized
on one of de two sides of a camera,
all the movies are exegesis-rated,
and parental babushkas are advised. (Dis not like Grace,
where spine-broke chairs, a dirt floor seasoned wid popcorn
—a proving ground for adolescent rats—
a bed-sheet screen in a tree-hung way be de place we go
to blast off for de planet of L.A.!)
Home of Storm Damage, of de siren celluloid.
She bend over, for which her audience deeply grateful.
She show us her bottom enclad in underpants,
for which she receive one point five million
and a percentage of de gate. She frequent Fat Farms.
("Would you like to *not* have another helping, Storm?"
"Yes, Dan, I wouldn't.") She go through husbands like casseroles.
To her Leading Man, Hoyo de Gracil, she say
"My love will last till they run out of film."
His fine china jaw and perma-tan

(he a sun worshiper of de third resolve)
frame a fragile coalition for a screen career.
In his last film he play an incredibly minor role.

America, an economy dat hum
like a hamper of flies, where the top line and the bottom
are in easy walking distance. Cause us to say,
Here is a cornucopia feeding on itself.
Home of Cornifed Foot Powder. ("Active ingredients?
Flour, soda, sand—we got no *active* ingredients.")
Major market for de Subaru Polyglue,
a car of mistaken proportions,
and de Yterba Accessa which feature,
instead of air bags, body bags.
Home of de Continental Fart Company, whose business be
to transport trailer trucks loaded wid Eastern farts
cross country to de California market.
In dis way de East balance its trade wid de West:
Something in return for de flow of agricultural próduce,
something in addition to money. De "semi" driver
responsible for topping off de load each day.

America, where de best rise
like ivy's always incompleted climb
(give it a grab of soil and watch it go).
Out of de See-and-Be-Seen multitude,
one rise like an arrowing black Gascony:
one Eddy Ubbjer, a young man who consider
bilious paperwork a long day in a tight collar.
For him no *VP of Perfunctory Affairs*
to *Senior VP in Charge of Surprises*
to *President,* standing in for God.

Instead he read the life of John D.
who said to the assembled millionaires
"It will take a hundred of you to fill the hole I leave."
Eddy listen for the quiet pump of money,
subterranean to all we do. In suits of banker blue
he go on the prowl for capital moves.
("Any calls? Messages? Vituperative asides?")
He do a dance of seven corporate veils.
He ride the creative curves of imbalance from Inc. to Inc.
He organize a company as a six-mile column of air.
The Ben Lee Bovine Erectile Tissue and Truck Depository
"Sand and Gravel—All You Can Eat"
His name, which he change to Imlicky Bayode,
become synonymous wid unfilled contracts. His slogan:
"I could do with more. I could do much more with more."
The Fairly Ferrous Metal & Metal Company
"Say It With Steel Castings"
His gold card he turn in for de coveted molybdenum card.
His power he manifest in box seats. (He listen
to tony music dat put him to sleep when no one looking.)
The Katie & Lytie Railway
The Nipsburg & Piton Railroad
The Ansveldt and Onslaught Railroad
He contrail the earth at seven altitudes.
On nodules of intricacy he fly above
the aqua lozenges of swimming pools.
He close deals over the *ponk* of a tennis ball.
Geomanque— "Serving Change Through Chaos"
He live at de material summit of de world.
("I add what I can to the mythologies of ownership.")
Money in the bank he call "the pleasure of potential,
the pleasure of choice." He build Hogey Castle

on Carmichael Heights: a flight of spires to give
the aeries above the Rhine a run for their money.
In a golden light the quarrels of his keep
promise a sunset made splendid by pollution.
*Communicare: A Health Company Specializing
in the Transmission of Communicable Diseases.*
He spa at de Rancho Libido, in the high holds
of de Nevada Dissimular:
("Is dis where we come to pretty much restore ourselves?")
He maintain a dazzling house account.
Wid Binky, his significant other, he make love
like a punch press, stamping machine, hydraulic ram.
Like a blank of native copper she take his shape.
Nights they watch the latest sci-fi: *Kookie-neé Horrendis-wa.*
He write a best seller on his recipe for taconite gumbo.
His ownership extend to the supertanker *Entropy Resolve.*
The Ohio & Oopslip Steamship Company
He address his Annual Meeting: "Ladies and Assumptions.
Two years ago I told you our goal
was just under $6 a share. Last year I told you,
'Enough fucking around. We going to bet the Company.'"
He tap his foot. He declare bankruptcy.
He say "This too will pass from corporate memory.
The thing about commerce is it doesn't care."
Of what come after I hear two accounts. One:
He march to the drumbeat of unsuccess.
Three, four times a day he beat his face wid martinis.
Chemically happy he was heard to say
"*Dis* will shake dem from their commuter *duh's*"
as he step in *front* of his arriving train.
In the alternate he have a change of heart
as massive as a embolism. He take vows,

he become ordained in *The Church of the Heavenly Circuit
of the Just Response.* He go to Rainbott and take de cure.
He get his teeth capped and a spiritual rejuvenation.
He found a church based on a six-mile column of air.
The Subsidy for the Sisters of Collision.
(Who would have thought, at his age, he would grow
this horn of character, this great tusk of concern?)

America, home of the Network News:
"Goodnight, Chet." "Goodnight, Logjam."
And the TV ad: "Watcha doin', Mom?"
"Making the house smell good."
(Then she spray her daughter in the face with Lysol.)
Home of de hit Soap *Mommy's Knee.*
(De audience must take TV fame for immortality
made visible; dey must hunger for humor.
At de merest of jokes dey laugh on and on.)

America? Home of *The Evening Poop*
where the news don't happen till you bring the paper home.
Where daily they beat the malleable metal of our emotions
into some new shape, under the editorial *thou*
serve up steaming piles of horse sense.
(In a country of spotlights wid not much to illuminate,
dere daily torrent of print on yesterday's mistakes
further de tyranny of de quotidian.
Helps us understand why newspapers
are printed on such flimsy stock.)
Journalists, descended from French fur trappers, seek
to absquatulate wid dere prey. When nothing better's doing,
dey feed on reputations. Always this side of salacious,
the search for truth is room by room.
Though gossip and slander never get loose in de compound,

truth-telling is an act of attrition and people die
of dere attention. Though all the news is fit to print
de *Corrections and Attractions* run for pages.
Souls of discretion, reporters wid Walter Winchells dangling
from dere lips type below a slow fanfare of smoke.
Warily dey regard de Maginot of editorial trenches.
The editors, practised at staying awake,
wait for the *Titanics* to find dere icebergs.
On a diet of sticky buns and hard copy
dey exercise a complex set of stopping rules.
A blue haze at a time dey smoke cigars. Dey say
"Around here we cry de Catch-Cries of de clown.
It help to have a pedantic exterior and a garbage mind."
The publisher in his office puff his pipe—warm bombs of smoke.
He straighten his plaque: POWER NOT PERMANENCE
He *write* the complex set of stopping rules.
He announce: "For the crime of mixing your media
the sentence is death by commutation."
He commend Kent Cub, pride of his paper, who
as a young man, seeking to be impressive by being outrageous,
wrote on shithouse walls. For his distinguished reporting
("Live-In Boyfriend Sets Pregnant Woman Afire"
and "Boy Wonder Rides Bike Down Up Escalator")
he earn his Pulitzer. In the fight for status as household name,
he in the encomium finals, the immortality playoffs.

America, home of New York's Poet Laureate.
"Hello, my name, Engarde Monocutter, is."
He de featured Sensibility of de Month.
Poetry editor for de New York telephone directory,
he have de naming rights for much of Manhattan,
but he in de hunt for opportunities beyond.
("Manhattan is a state of mind.
I live in a cave at the northern tip,

on Vespucius Creek — the Harlem River to you.")
He decline to be sized, to step into the portrait
people make of him, to entrap him wid context.
His audience he address as "Gringo and Gringesse."
Instead of "Fabulous" he say "Fablioux."
From his latest book, *The War of Jenkin's Ear,*
he quote a line "surpassing Shakespeare's:
Oh never, never, never, never, never, *never.*"
He working on an epic called *Vito's Underpants*
which he describe as "de flip side of Ovid."
You'll find dis book, which he call a turbulence of verse,
to be "where the rubber meets de road."
"It's a formal work — which mean if things get slow
you can study the rhyme for deeper meaning."
Based on the lexicon of elevator logic,
in a great gross of lines it seek to make
a linearity of sense of de universe.
In the face of hub and bub, it poultice and enfranchise.
It chant a dealy enclaimer. It begin:
Gesthemane Gals, won't you come out tonight,
come out tonight, come out tonight?
Its conclusion, unavoidable as a road kill,
is unmitigated in its gall.

    "I know I am — *eehew!* — supposed to give you
long lariatal loops of feedback on your life.
With regard to Art as a high calling, however,
I am here to pee on Walter Pater's campfire.
Instead of High Art, it going to be Hi, Art."
The poet he describe as one who is
attached to life by a different set of hooks.
The poet he compare to a man in a Men's Room
peering into those opposing mirrors:
his business is dis parliament of images.

He call the essential figure of the poet
"a man in a dump, holding a broken lamp
—a white porcelain fracture of the made—
gripping it like significance." He say,
"As I have said elsewhere in my literature,
the job of the poet is to sojourn and report.
To ride the creative curves of imbalance from ink to ink."

The poet's job: To gambit on the high relaxer,
                 to allure the fragrant bias,
                 to cozzen the fiddly mailleau.
                 To hit a rhapsodic counterpoint,
                 to paderewski the blind epogue,
                 to engineer the rude awakening.
                 To implode the aussi,
                 to make a global hullabaloo,
                 to sicklebar for glory.

(His own work he decline to read except to say
"It's new and it's true. Not borrowed, not blue.")

    Poetry should be hurricanal: a quiet seeking eye
in the midst of gale-force disturbances. It should
report tectonic events, continental shifts of the self.
It should be as natural as stalagmites
and other things that accrete in the dark. It should meet
a standard of entertainment as well as resonance.
"Laments, gatherings, salutes: I can hear the bourdon and skirl."
(His own work he decline to read
for reasons of sublimity.)

    Modern poetry he call a toxic waste dump.
American poetry, a glum tostada.
American poets, "for the most part a slovenly, misplaced lot.

One half the watch is sick on deck, the other half below.
But they are happy to serve as acrostics;
Frost reveled over such things." Poetry prizes:
"Autocratic crud. Fair play they regard as foreplay."
(His own work he decline to read
"due to excesses of the night before.")

    I take some notes on de Q & A.
"Yes"
"No"
"No"
"The answer is Of Course. The consequence, of course, be No."

Q. 'garde, what about Thanatopsis Sorelink?
A. The author of *Wellington's Beef?* Fresh off the nonsense farm,
the satellite dish farm. He a poet not of the modernist suburbs.

Q. Emile Trope?
A. An erudite patronne. May I quickly footnote my regard.
A book at a time, he mutter a slow exhaust of words.

Q. McChesney Daffenwhat?
A. As a writer of substantive twaddle from Loyola, he have
de repressible bletch. He take his bearings from de moon.

Q. 'garde, tell us about the nature of radioactivity.
A. "   "

Q. What about Shat Waddell?
A. To him the charges seem inevidential.
From such disturbance he himself eloign.

48

Q. April Flung?
A. Poetry is too important to be polite about.
She have the predator's wonderful nose.
She show us why *auteur* and amateur have de same root.

Q. Henry Continuoso?
A. He give his muse a scratchy fidelity. I call
his work summer drainage, a pile of well-done Well Done.

Q. Eppletawny Swinglesnot?
A. His be a street-felt poetry, a warren of indirection.

Q. Asbeck Rohatbeck?
A. Always able to get a poem published. An example of poets
and editors dealing in poems dat clear each other's markets.

Q. I was wondering if you'd care to comment
on my new book *Bygones & By Goners?*
A. I will have to add dat one to the "Must Reads,"
a subsection of the "Not Going to Reads."

Q. Dudwiller Inscrutiballi?
A. De secret of metaphoric activity, I agree,
consist in leaving de side doors open, but Inscrutiballi write
wid de confidence of one who counts on being misunderstood.

Q. Randy Grandiloquence?
A. He writing the Great American Pleurisy.
He dictate poems—long panels of verse—like office memos.
He will be buried wid a dictaphone in his crossed palms.

Q. Recently I read three books of poetry:
one about de agonies of old age; one about
bombed-out Ireland; one about a dead father. 'garde,
how you rouse an entire profession out of a bad mood?
A. You must accept poetry as one of de subcutaneous arts.

Q. Academics?
A. What they do with their half of the magic is their business.
(Literary criticism he call
a subpart of de gaming industry.)

Q. Would you care to comment on the state of critical aplomb?
A. In priestly fashion dey man the barricades.

Q. Jules Oxnibbitude?
A. He take de part of de poets who track dere times
and write from soulful pits, but never cop awards.
He take dem by de hand. He bless dem.

Q. 'garde, what about the New Factotums?
A. Know-Nothings in the business of nurturing their own
sensibilities. They write beautifully, have nothing to say.

Q. I was reading de Tocquiville recently—
you know, for a little intellectual roughage—when I thought,
I should ask 'garde about The Belligerents.
A. A street regime. The grime is palpable.
A company of bezoinkers.

Q. The New Transvestites?
A. Quick inks. They give their little genes a shake
to ask if there is some mistake.

Q. Recently a critic, one William Equity,
called your work "a Highland doggerel"
and "a descent into mere virtuosity."
He describe a number of your books — *The End of Cadence,*
The Flooded Tuba, The Onion Bin, The Journey to Attention —
as a kind of Decameron of bad taste. Could you comment?

A. To this Monocutter discharge like a rusty
musket of a caliber beyond what one might expect.
He try for a Bohemian brain-shot.
Dis "critic," a fat boy on a found farm,
take punditry as pretense to new highs.
His style is — you know — to be at once
both very folksy and totally wrong.
He writes in physically eruptive sentences.
He is an ego that walks on all fours and hunts by night.

Q. I am William Equity. And in fact I called you
"the visible freak of an addicted nomenclature."
I compared you as artist to the alligator,
who shits in his own medium.

A. "Izzatso?", Monocutter say. And "Izzatright?"
Den wid a Rotweiller imprecision dey go at it.
Equity land a savage Dexter; like Byron
he cause club-footed mayhem on de upper decks.
Monocutter turn the retaliatory tables;
he knock Sweet William down and he told him so.
Like a scuffle wid thieves dey roll on de floor
in a distribution of saliva, a redistricting
of teeth, a settlement — tit-for-tat — of *peristroyka.*

Blood spatter de tattersall. 'garde sit up, spit out
from fretted gums a broken few ansigular teeth.
He offer to punch out William's literary lights.
William, his face a forced devolvement of indigos and browns,
offer to send 'garde forever into the sonnety darkness.

America, home of Spillman Sponneker,
who come to attention when he declare
"I am a citizen of de world. And dat include Bayonne."
He leave his job as clerk in Ladies Underludes
("You will find him in *Unmentionables*,
right next to *Unspeakables*.") to seek office.
He run an eglacklier campaign based on careful claims.
A bustle of attitudes, he out there mouthing platitudes
the livelong day, standing for things three at a time,
promoting virtues as hard to find as last month's newspaper.
His platform: *Dis a very strange and exciting time.*
His slogan: *A branch for every bird dat got a song to sing.*
He campaign against de taxpayer's aneurysm.
He make considered shouts of protest.
He declare against those "who greet ideas
with the Boy Scouts' preferred method of putting out campfires."
He inveigh against "Politics,
dat most cynical of bespeakals."
He cascade into office on de cry "Alright!
We gonna be all things to all people!"
Ward by ward he learn his politics.
He yearn for de decibel power of de P.A., de franking
privilege, to use widout mercy on his constituents.
Many were those who wrote him off, who say "He will,
you can be assured, fail into prominence."

But in a master stroke which confound his critics
he declare Bayonne a state, the Union's fifty-first,
by virtue of its charter which include, as an afterthought,
"and all other lands not otherwise appurtenant to or claimed by."
Alleyways in Kenosha, six inches of curbing in the Bronx,
surveyors' remnants and mistakes cause this to be
the country's third largest state in land area if not in population.
("Gerrymandered" is the word that could have found
its destiny in describing the state of Bayonne
but for the fact that its existence was the result
of imperfect maps, not the cause of them.)
The administration of Governor Sponneker consist of himself,
one secretary and 433 class action attorneys.
The secretary earn his office when he emerge
from cardboard housing on a 4 x 120 foot
strip behind a Cincinnati mall
to found The Henderson Boundary Company. He give
the Governor his vision of a spoiler's strategy.
Injunctions against property developers,
the threat of competing bids from the State, the threat
of Imminent Domain and a winning record in court
brought per capita GNP to a level
second only to the State of Saudi Arabia.

    The Governor dopen his constituents. "Of dat
he couldn't say for sure." "His response to dat is in de file."
Grown heady wid avoidance he declare
for Congress, home of master backslappers
(*maybe* even Sneaker of de House).
He seek to loom large in de histories.
With supporters numbered in the scads, he grip the gladdenhand,

he run on de Vainglory ticket for de coveted second term.
"Unaccustomed as I am to public emptiness,
dere is a freshness dat come wid public trust renewed."
Like TooLoose-Lautrec he promise incompatibility,
like the *New York Post* incorruptibility and a late edition.
Democracy he call "A urinal placed four feet up de wall:
it do the job but it's hard to use." Of freedom
he speak quite some number of ennobling words.
Bit bad by de bug, he dream of running for the Big One.
(At his Inaugural he say, "Abe Lincoln say,
You can fool all of the people some of the time.
You can fool some of the people all of the time.
Among these he did not express a preference,
but unless you a President or Madonna, the first choice
don't come up. For the rest of us,
the second seem the better way to go.")
He wish to be remembered as de Seat Belt President.
"I got de country to wear it." He entertain
legislation to make of his mind a national park.
Like a stuck record he'll be remembered for how he malfunctions.

America, a land wid an evolving definition of wrong
cause us to say "Whatever happened to the last priest?"
America, home of de Contemptible Bede,
pastor of de First Church of Congoleum
(the Reverend Gracie de Beau presupposing),
who pause in his sermon on nationwide TV—
a wide smile breach his face, between his teeth
he bear a continental divide—to proclaim
dat he will put aside de black frock and gold chain

and move out of his air-conditioned *Amenhop*
and lead his flock out of the land that speak for itself.
Out of de valley of de shadow of after-tax violence,
where people run from de liquid part of de rain
and cities are a continuous buffeting of crusts.
His people he will lead West, to a land of premise.
To the country's cathodic, garnet-packed interior,
to the be-Christed summits of the Nevada Dissimular.
There in the high holds of the mitred summits to found
a cityhood for God. Dere each will feed
according to his need, like Bengladesh at its best.
His flock he teach to pray in de following manner:
I pledge adherence to the flag
of the extended State of Euphoria,
and to the indulgence toward which it leans,
one notion, in sympathy and semen forever.
His notional anthem: *Rally 'Round de 'Rousal Tree.*
"And our society will be decorous.
Although our citizens will walk about
wid genitals on full display,
dere heads dey will hide in carefully-fitted bags
in what is merely another kind of modesty.
An organ other than the heart will be our central metaphor.
Monogamy will give way to Impulse Shopping.
("You'll find him down at the mating pole today,"
or "She was last seen down at the breeding barns.")
Instead of socializing over meals young lovers
will meet for a fecal tryst; families will gather
at the latrine; the occasion for conviviality
not what we eat but what we make of what we eat."

To the scads of white-robed faithful in the hall
the Bede then make his Altar Call: for a few volunteers
("women incredibly procreative and intentive,
chosen for their range of breeding habits"),
and for support ("Our prayer lines are open.
If you've received a blessing from this broadcast,
send us a blessing in return. God loves a cheerful giver.").
Years later the Bede was found drinking
the last glass of water in Tucson, after which he became
an arcade seminarian, a declamatory hod, a watchtower noddy.
He change his name to de Virtuous Cashpur, de Eligible Pon.
Late in life he became quite cosmopolitan
and was off-putting in a wide variety of situations.

America? It's a carve of a continent,
a known fleeing place for felons,
home of de now-ubiquitous Maybe plant.
America? It's pretty round, pretty flat.
Except for New York City, which be pointy.

I been to New York. Once.
Manhattan Island be de terrapin of Indian myth.
Man steel his commerce on de colossal fossil
of his granite hull. I seen de Navajos creep
a skypooper's skeletal skin, 50 stories up,
shelterin' in dere hands blue bits of arc,
tryin' to build a fire. But de girders never catch.
(Close up I seen one, through black glass communing with his spark.
He follow de smoking idea of its bead, de slow
progress of its wake as it wander de metal's face.)

Dey bundle the turtle space wid interstates.
The overpass, 9' 7", hold open like a mouth,

the next, 9' 8", hold open like a mouth.
Cars outrunning the rust erupting from their trunks,
asphalt trucks, flat beds, milk tankers:
Welcome to de Cavalcade of Commerce!
Airports launch old Boeings like grand asides.
Barges weave wakes on its periphery.
But the tortoise hold his course dead slow.
In due time we will know whether up the Hudson
he will head or by the Sound to sea he'll go.

        I been to New York. Once.
Commuters there be cut out of 1940's cloth.
They leave their dark apartments,
wallpaper clinging to the walls,
pictures grasping their hooks.
Armed wid candied armpits, polished breath,
dey are buttoned at points of stress.
Dey are beveled like plate glass mirrors.
Dey are balanced like the rules of chess.
Dere train arrive pulling its wind behind
like a brief history. Dey grab for seats.

        Used as directed, dere unused portions are returned,
hauled through twilight in a hard doze.
In dere dream an addict say "I have a need
dat stand outside this conversation.
For heavenly Nicaraguan bales."
And they: "My life is moving on graphs.
They are reading the labels in my clothes.
The ecstatic mugger with my wallet
finds it easy to be me." The train
emit green shocks along the right-of-way.

Well up the ladder of apparent happiness
dey go to an ordered acre and its home
of timbered Tudor, storied stone.
Some of dem appear to hit de Lotto.
On long Petrarchan drives to weekend lakes
dey rest from de frenzy of possessing.

I been to New York. Once.
No government steakhouse where de only customers
come in by mistake, where de hair in your salad
have a twist of pubic vigor,
at *The Selective Pâté* dey feature Extinctive Dining.
Dey seat you to a ring-around of glass.
Dey serve you butter by de double pat.
Dey scrub de spoons till nothing visible is left.
So clean you wouldn't think of it
if they did not, with tongs dey serve you bread.
Dey serve Imaginatively Salted Almonds and wine,
which they describe as a potable libation to the gods.
Barely to the rise of the round, they fill the glass:
stemmed, it uphold its ball of Chardonnay
to be candled for its year of cider light.
De waiters dere enjoy each other's company,
with customers maintain bilateral accord.
Dey move among de crowd, dere wooly testicles at ease.
Dey pride themselves on a snappy repartee.
("How you eat it is up to you.") To patrons asking water
dey invoke de diplomat's immunity.
They name the Specials of the Day—all off-menu—
as unrepeatable opportunities.

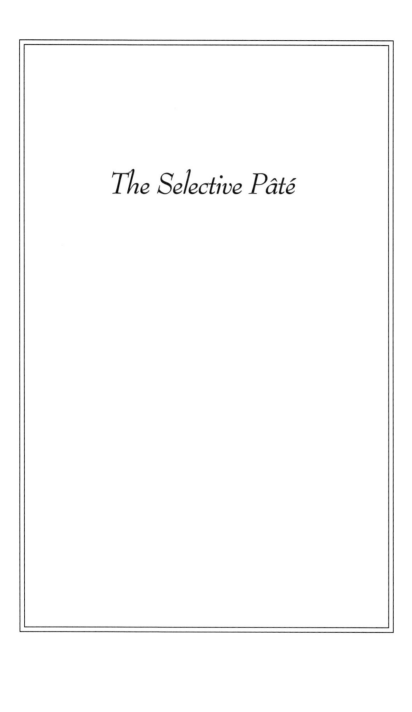

The Selective Pâté

— To Begin —

Caviar.	A relish wid a garnish.
Snails.	Hulled and steamed on a bed of privet.
Lump Ovoid Cocktail.	On cracked ice.
Eggs Arbuthnot.	Progeny of frog, boiled quick in the string and served as a mêlée of pasta.
The Basta Caliente.	Gazpacho suitable for chumming.
The Pasta Caliente.	In the great chorus of flavors, this one spaghetti.
Savouries of Lemur.	Defeased from de mother's purse.
A Dish of Clamour.	Purloin of pig bowel, served on a souvenir plate.
The Daily Express.	A prune flush for the hard of having, for those who have been rear-ended recently.
Crudité,	which speak for itself.

— For Fish —

A gather of brook twaddle.	Served on a bed of neglect.
Our bouillabaisse.	A resonance of cod, grouper, snapper, grinder, wrangler, bungler.
Malignancies of Sea Slug.	Served wid a biopsy report.
A hatch of kippers.	Seined from de crapper.

—For Flesh—

Fried Guzzle.	If you in de hunt for grease; if your genes have a cockroach twist.
Megachamber Pie.	Hearts of sheep, goat, llama in a paisley crust.
Flaming Testicles.	Served wid a knowing smile.
The Safe Landing.	A loaf of protein for the aerodynamically aware.
Remonstrance of Quail.	A cock and hen taken at the height of their indignation.
Chicken Disappointment.	Something you might as well get used to.

Period of Hog.	*Heightened with chutney, heavy on the Greek effoud.*
A trick of rabbits.	*Hauled from the hutch, eared on the spot.*
A Scare	
of Young Monkey.	*Steamed in the knapsack, served intact.*
A Gnaw of Boar.	*Reduced in a crucible.*
Aged Upshot.	*Served with an Attaboy; payable in advance.*
The Haggis.	*Served with rights to aftercare.*
A Joint	
of Happenstance.	*Served at gunpoint.*
The Big Sleep.	*Delivered with a fist containing a roll of dimes.*
Mother Fucker Stew.	*Prepared in the Bronx under our direction.*

—For the Salad— *

Sanctimonious Salad.	*A simple salad, made with an effort, served with a sneer.*
Roulette of Salade.	*A dive of endive, a swish of lettuce, a spring of parsley and Voila!*
De Hungry Planet.	*A head of cabbage in a glaze of cold cream.*

* *We have Bleu Cheese and all de Ready-to-Wear sauces.*

—The Just Dessert—

Frozen Cusp.	*From our dairy vaults.*
Mucilage Pie.	*A garbanzo clot which the waiter will be happy to argue about.*
The Chef's Surprise.	*Served with apologies depending on his mood.*

Our service is compris but any extra is welcome to defray de cost of savagery.

You say you just ate. "A whole bayou
of *Invidio Parsnip*. A bog of cranberries.
Potato chips and white wine, dat will be quite fine."

I been to New York. Once.
Used the facilities in de Port Authority.
Looked up to hear, from a hole in de ceiling,
a voice surrounded by a face: "Hello from de plenum.
Did you leave some in dere for me?"
Stayed at Delmore's Bed & Bucket. De roaches dere
have heart transplants and know de use of steroids.
But dis be better dan de man who live
in a wine press, grapes of wrath his daily fare.
Who sing full-bore on de street,
giving his unseen enemies de lie.
Beat the drummer who, drumless, tatoo the skin of 53rd.
Beat de obese, ragged man clapping
on de corner of Radio City Music Hall:
"I'm getting my applause done early."
Beat de addict working—a work in progress—on his death.
Wid a spoon and match he make a little needle song,
he stick it in de native blood supply.
He say "I got a heroin abduction."
Dey walk de streets like screws worked loose,
dey make self-portraits wid dere remarks.
(Some say dey got radios in dere heads,
dey merely repeating what dey hear.)
But mere additional definitions of failure dese
are not. Dere is an authenticity to the thralls
in which dey are held. Dey are prices paid.
Dis why madness, if not noble, can be divine.
Dey walk around like misnomers.
Dey show up like a furtive meal-ticket;
at fancy restaurants dey look in like a shabby *sir*.
Dey know de efficacious smell of garbage on a summer morn,
de Hail-and-Well-Met of microbes in a compost heap.
Dey find new ways to stay alive, strategies
for survival dat do not depend on mind.

Wid pan-fried brains, dey do a vegetable hustle.
Dey do the work of windshield *blumps*, at stop lights
drivers say "Look at that man be hungry."
Dey inspect de Kimbell of litter
(a high-class trash, not like the tired dump of Grace);
a nickel at a time dey build de family fortune.
If one fall in wid thieves, dey ouch him and dey scotch him,
dey leave him for a goner. In the repose of the needy,
dey lie down stress-free on de sidewalk, dey pass the night
at the Inn of No Kidding & No Forgiving.
De guests here lie around like scattered amendments,
scattered returns. De men sleep fetal, hands in laps,
to protect dere Foucault Pendulums
from outside grabbers of dere gravity.
Patrolmen test wid night sticks de integrity of skulls,
de answerability of feet. From a full city block
de voices reckon, dey descant for de hard of hearing.
Come summer dey lodge in bombed-out cars, an edge
of overhang, anything more top than bottom, when
"This be a revery rain. And this be a drool.
And here come a dump of glittering tons."
Come winter dey live on de given heat of subways.
Whole flagrants of newsprint dey use to line
dere clothes, for it insulate like nothing.
Widout de leather hulls our feet call home,
widout our soles of oxen groan,
our fur coat solutions to the frost,
dey grow slumbery in cold. Dey enter a crystal
dormancy. Of no account, dey freeze and drop off.

III. THE OPPOSITE NUMBER

W E DEALING HERE with the downstream issues
        of Adam and Eve:
de fangle of de feminine, de procreative surge,
de universal condition of insufficient nooky.
I think you know dat reproduction, Geode,
is de strategy dat Nature hit upon
as a way for living kinds to hang around.
A kind of immortality by proxy

for de individual, albeit a poor second
to his own succumb as far as he concerned.
You've seen de business of de barnyard, how dogs
all smell and smell alike in dere democracy of tails.
How critter kine amble and mount like mammal tonnage.
How frog on frog inseminate plasmodic eggs.
The aphid, born gravid, in three days double its kind — or would,
were it not wheat to the nation of de scything ant.
Chordate mother say to chordate fry:
Get out there on the reef and breed.
For dis be the pro(explosion)iferation,
de steaming underbake, dat underlie the world.

   Reproduction help de individual
to deal wid de fact of his demise. And, too,
to have some fun along de way. But I myself
find intercourse a strange mucilage to bind
a species to existence. Perhaps you think, like me,
if children are the end den sex is an unlikely means.
Puts parents in an awkward spot: How *can* dey walk around
wid all dese confessions of intercourse?
Why not just instill in man an ardor for offspring?
Why not put some pollen on a pistil on a stem
and, like de overshafted tulip, let us whelp on de breeze?
(The daffydil, wid its deeply meaningful sexual parts,
pose de question to passers-by. Wid questions
of its own, here come de honey bee.)
If sex to be retained for pleasure, why den define it
broadly: "A coming together for a purpose. A coalition."
Make most of de body an erroneous zone.
Perhaps, you think, the glands are well-positioned
for protection but not for ease of access.
You imagine de antics necessary to engage —

400 positions for a start—and I agree.
(Perhaps you think the Maker, having invented the sperm,
say "Now We've got to figure a way to deliver it.")
You'd think, if the aim is to persuade an appendage
to do double duty as a sperm gun,
Nature could do better dan mixing up
the sperm count wid de urinary flows.
One could achieve de necessary intercourse,
for example, by a vigorous shaking of de hands.
De rigid middle finger already serve dis purpose
for social intersay. Only trouble,
you'd be eatin' popcorn wid your penis
and in de arousal state you wouldn't be able to write.
More often than now, you'd catch your penis in de door.
No need for urinals as such...need to be careful,
though, lickin' de fingers or pickin' de nose,
to avoid self-arousal. Dat must be why Nature
choose your penis to be its two-way switch.
So Nature, to achieve what She found necessary,
would make of mating dis chaotic enterprise.
Strange to de point of strange, this extraordinary rite.
In its predictability and perfectability,
almost a ritual; in its spontaneity
not like a ritual at all. At once
voluntary and involuntary. At once
urgent and comical, cogent and chemical.
Like water, essential to life but widout calories.
Your look suggest you having some trouble wid de concept.

　　Suppose you walkin' down the road one day,
when who should amble up but Amber Wunt.
You remember her, young, to have de souvrain polyps
and rudderless void. For brains, she at de poverty line,

but from an early age she exhibit sexual comprendo.
Today she have a face to make de sybarites sing.
And she dressed for presentation. Plumped
in de fabric hold of a nictitating *peau de soie*
she walk wid a considerable jiggle; the wind
flap the flag of her skirt, ah oh. Oh ah.
It put you in mind of her pelvic stance,
the inward tow of her *tell*, her gentle divides.
You look down to see your folly, normally the size
of bucket bait, is now de size and shape of a trout.
She invite you to her place "to join in de fight for birthright."
Dere will be a meeting at her home, she say,
for purposes of discussing internal combustion.
On dis trip, she say, your head is not invited.

    Not quite sure of the cause, at eight you arrive.
"Check your heart at the door," she say,
"but bring the rest in, definitely."
Dressed for access, she cavalcade de peignoir.
She want to be your brash companion.
She begin to unwrap de codicils.
You whoa de horses but she reveal her stunning asides.
(When a woman takes off her top, Geode,
it's always a moment in the history of the world.)
The sight of her aureoles focus your mind wonderfully.
You begin to perspire from de tops of your feet.
She ask if you know de touch of woman flesh.
You couldn't say for sure. Dat's pretty soft, you say.
(The soft side of a female breast,
this one thing the mammal gene do best.)
"Do you do," she say, "the moist embark?"
She visit on you the shaped autocratics
of her mouth. You love crush her in return.
"Can you feel randy?" she say, and she display de out takes.

68

De violins in your head go *squeakle squeakle.*
"I like a considerable, a totemic hang," she say,
"but now we gonna take de swingle out of de dickle."
Slowly she draw your folly from its holster hold.
She watch the fellow's slow unslumber.
Under her gaze, it lose its limber camber.
It grow in her hand like a good investment.
It gain a mind of its own and soon, a will.
From Peter the Recluse, Peter Recumbent, Peter Couchant
to Peeking Peter, Peter the Great, Peter Magnificat!
You feel a need to knead her body like bagpipes,
to savage de nylon filigree, to make of her garden
a rapid salad, to reach into her like a creel.
You show a terrible aspect, ready to attack.
She so workmanlike. She delete your expletives.
Under the prolonged coaching of her grip
("*I'll* give you a couch potato."),
she teach you emission control. She bring you to brinkage,
to de point of maximum spendiole.
To her hearty affirmations of *Uh Huh,*
you render your octane load: of your life
the ten thousand six hundred fifty-third.

   "Oh well enough, well enough," you say. "OK.
But I can leave it well enough alone. I'll clip
remember coupons and I'll say *No Thanks* to dat.
My peenwa, thank you very much, will have to learn
to live alone in its hermitage of underpants."
You try to live a life not bad,
enough food, enough sleep, when — WOW —
Where is dat testosterone comin' from?
Stronger dan a pint of hemoglobingobblegavin
administered intranervously, more potent dan 3 cc's
of ohtentribe dyhixxadribble taken infernally.

You join dose for whom, compared to sex,
all else is second, third, last. Dat rat pack of neurons
called your pizzle outdo itself in speaking for us all.
Days on end you live at de end of your dick.
Nothing will do but it must be your slipknot
to eternity. As if de only bit of antimatter
in our galaxy has come to rest on its head.

    The libido, Geode, is a creature who live in a well.
Sometimes when you go to haul up water,
you get him instead. Then, like a familiar
in the watches of the night, he walk the land.
He sit in the moonlight on your patio,
a man in overcoat and hat. He enter your room
and stand at your bed. He say, *I mean you harm.*
He drink wild waters. Everywhere he look he see
the obverted *O'dell,* the ensculpted *aroo,*
the huge *nethingness* of *narcoltwist,*
until the rest of the body seem simply a set of approaches
—couloirs and combes—to the female point of it all.
In the grip of his unregulated flesh, a man become
unvalved. His peenwa he brandish like a death-tool.
(I myself have given rise to jillions of intemperate sperm.)
Everything is a Rorschach blot—even the moon
look like Venus de Smilo—until the only thing
you see: golden magnums, bicameral legs and groin lock.
Man's life, dey say, is solitary, poor,
nasty, brutish and short. To dat I would add "horny."
This need for congress come to us by ancient authority—
Pliny, Horace, Vichyssoise—soft-scored, morocco-bound.
The libido be like a storm in a bottle. Each of us
must decide to let it out a little or a lot. Or not.
Den you learn de unsafety of trying to live your fantasies.

Suppose you walkin' down de road one day,
a guerrilla on de borders of hopefulness,
when you pass a girl who sport a brush cut
in de fashion of de day. From de back
she might be boy but from de front, never.
Like a bullshot in a pinball she hit
every post in de screen of your mind:

10,000!   BONUS POINTS!   FREE GAME!

You look down to see dat your land's end, which normally
hang like Manhattan from de pelvis of New York,
now occupy de space reserved for Long Island.
Your iffer, on de Fangle Index, rise to 10.
Your body think it know just what to do.
Question is, How you broach her posy integrity?
She at de pixy interlude
and may not be so ready to engage.
She not going to *invite* your carroty encumber.
She not simply going to plant her body in a laird
allure and say "Come stop my continental drift."
If you walk up you'll get dat "What do *you* want?" stare.
You can't just say "Dat be a hat-sized Geronimo"
and ask her for the Evermore Enough,
or you'll risk de little serpent of her tongue,
you'll get that "Don't you *ever*" ploy. You can't just say
"Excuse my rampant nakedness" and present yourself
as a bar presents its bartender: standing behind it.
You can't just kneel to the próduce of thighs,
and examine the nether grimace, the meats of yë.
Most certainly you can't just take her by de baffles.
If you assume dat ladies all be consenting adults —
"You know better, you just forget to ask." —

dat can be a chaotic embrace. Dat can be known as rape.
(Statutory rape? Dat be out dere in de dark
committin' felony wid de marble fawns and bronze reliefs.
You can think of it as statuary grope—
unnatural acts wid Sgt.York.)

    No, you can't just plumb de savvy atcher.
You can't just grab dem by de nummulospheres.
You must turn de acrids of desire
into a certain sassy sap.
You must turn *resolve* into *adroit*
and butternut her autonomy.
In short you must learn to Lothario.
You must know when to flutter wid praise
and when to deplore de subway service.
You must applaud politely at de polo grounds
and *Tsk Tsk* at de *Evening News* when "Dis abet de shiftless!",
dey decry. And you must *never* let on
dat de only thing dat's on your mind,
is to dip your cruller in de lady's cup of Joe.
Now you would think dat ladies get de same apply as men.
But no, dey seem to sit, day after day,
dere hair just so, dere mesh in place,
dere perfume ranged in veils around dem,
dere phenomes and pharamones deployed like lures.
Puts us trout in a fractious position.
We hit de bait, we liable to end up here.
So something somewhat complicated going on,
wid most of de breeding going on behind closed doors.

    Suppose you angle and you finally get a date
with Claudine Wrangle, de girl of your dreams.
Claudine got de beginning of a chinker chin

and she puttin' some meat on de thigh, but she got
a plunging surf line and mammoth rejoinders. Since you lack a car
dis be a double date with Rehab Hodewald.
(He endure the trial by fire — he go to high school;
now he teach knots at de Marlybone Academy.)
His date be de Knockout of Knockerteague, Estelle de Minemouth.
She got piezoelectric crystals and de not-so-subtle transformer.
Locally she famous for introducing topspin to the game.
Now Rehab drive his car unsheathed, de radio —
"*Dat's* my music! *Dat's* my mood-suiting blues!
I could make a *meal* of dat!" — he play at full.
Out of Placenta Junction dere be a degree of road dust,
pollen and afterlife and such. After a couple of brews
he pull up under a junk of flowering arbuthnot
and he get out. As he unzip, a hand of wind
shower him wid a rain of sappy essence.
We hear "Now it's my turn, you augmitious bitches."
In the aisle of headlights a bright blade of pee
walk the dead leaves, loud as a stone crab.
He come back, zipping, wid de comment, "Sucker's heavy."
He tell Estelle to shake hands wid de unemployed.
Now dey engage in horseplay of de deep chuckle variety.
You hear Estelle, "This will put some lead in your pencil."
And he, "You have its complete attention. You giving me varicose veins."
Toying wid de outer reaches of de birth canal,
he extol de joys of spelunking as a sport.
Meanwhile you play Claudine de lonesome fiddle.
She have a cold. You palpable your regret.
You Gene Autry your courtly concern.
Rehab know from de feel of de buttons in de dark
which way is up. He pretend to read labels:
Affix Postage Here   Refrigerate After Opening
You say "After a few days does your shirt get slightly malignant?"

You say "Every week I take a shower to keep de scent down."
In de front seat we hear "Well grind my gears."
and "Watch out, you'll get blasted in the piastre."
We hear intermittent grunts, de usual inarticulates.
We sense deep-seated satisfaction.
In de back, your conversation gridlock. You recall
a Latvian sing-along. You down to remnants of prayers.
In front dey discuss a palomino dismount.
Pretty soon, Claudine, she in de front seat, too.
You hear, "Finally we got plenty to go around.
A man get lost in all de spare parts."
You talk a wobely sepulcher. You say,
"Dat one, dat's de Folio Bird. He petition de peaceable dark
wid Oleo. Oleo." Now de whole car shake.
You say, "Dat one, dat's de Mas-o-Minus Bird.
He cruise de eleemosynary air.
Stupid as a poet, he sing what's said."
And Rehab crow, "There will be a brief
intermission while I fuck the dog."

    After a time, Geode, you come to realize
dat matrimony—courtship and marriage—is de way
provided our kind to carry out Nature's strategy.
You dream of finding de woman of your dreams.
She will enter a room in all her ladyness.
She will curve and come to you as the air's blue mantle
come to earth: as finery, raiment, a delft of de soul.
In fine scarves and wooly chafferniks
she will carry her female otherness.
"Inveigle me," she will say, "wid word clusters devoid of sense."
Everything will smell of subduction and calico.
All you can think of is her confederate mouth.
In a moment of truth as big as a wedding you propose:

the two of you to come together as one.
You honeymoon on de Isle of Angus,
between the Visibles and the Invisibles.
Much of the civilized world is there.
At the Angiosperm Repulse couples emerge
from dere rooms in a closeness cause you to know,
before breakfast dey celebrate dere marriage again.
In de evening in de dining room,
the tables are little salt stations in the wind.
You can, if you listen carefully,
hear the semen dripping on the floor.
In the darkness that live always under covers
she pose herself around you, a willing coil.
As the invisible leader six times find its way
around itself to secure the hook's flake,
line and line you make the Angler's Knot.
This is the glory in its featherhold,
the deep Slavonic comfort dat Nature never told you about.
Together you rise to the mammal melting point.
You do and she do the unrivaled arch of ecstasy.
You happen like thunder over her;
she happen like earthquake under you.
As a plane lands in New Jersey's industrial dark,
as a float plane lights on Loon Lake,
you come down and she come down; together
you come down like domestic tranquility.
And after, you be to her a slumbery penumbra.
And after, may-hap, she will lap your head
and sing you a slumbery egg song. Or vice versa if you like.
You join de ranks of de inexpressibly content.
The two of you billow into residential flame.
You look forward to a household like a homily:
to shared pet peeves, little buttcake familiarities.

"Good night, Square Peg." "Good night, Round Hole."
You divide responsibilities:
she will be in charge of de family's spiritual well-being;
you will be in charge of its material well-being and libido.
Dis is how you dream it to be.

In the event it could be otherwise. You meet and marry.
("I pronounce you Matter and Anti-Matter.") Your wedding night,
your bride be ready for sexual matriculation.
Her mouth be a well of invitation,
her tongue in its cave ready to do business.
You hold her in a grip dat defy cooperation.
Your intrusion become self-sustaining, like internal combustion.
The two of you become a cooping and wheezing machine,
de purpose of which is less than obvious, a wobbling
and groaning machine, although to what end is not so clear.
She gasp quite a bit and she upheaval.
You reach a jittery completion,
you do a quiet molt of ecstasy.
Dere's not a lot left, when it's over, to say.
You offer a mossy metaphor. Back home,
you enter the temperate zone of dis relationship.
She settle down to the thankless task of re-inventing her husband;
you look forward to years of rolling on the floor
in a deep couple, to the quiet wet work of two.
Pretty soon, though, she prone to a natural disinterest.
"Please," she say, wid a lightest breaking of de voice,
"not too much love." Three nights in a row
she go to bed wid headaches. Quicker dan you can say
"De muffin is ready," you go from daily
to every-other-daily to almost-neverly.
Wid a *Not* and a *Now* you realize you just been disagreed with.
For a while your marriage keep its kilterstones in key.

76

But after a time of submissive tonic, she begin
to strike a dominant seventh. She open the day
with legion disapprovals, the morning tableau of demands.
In dis you see how "marital" and "martial"
become confused spellings of one another,
how "marital" become inseparable from "spat."
At breakfast she ask if you straightening up the house again,
having a symmetry attack. You ask "Is she
upstairs again, deciding if she be pretty today?"
She say she been busy planning her anger for the day.
You raise a recurrent concern, how your sex life rather
incompletely realized. Sex after marriage,
in fact, is something you've heard about but never had.
For her, she say, making love has joined the family
of highly repetitive acts. Dis you know: so unresponsive
has she become you've thought of dialing 911
to say: "I think my wife is dead." You discuss
your need to be together for purposes of congress:
what de civilized world call feeling horny.
"You mean," she say, "the enfilial entwango?
The furrowed épalpe, the intaglio entire?"
In having sex, you say, dere doesn't seem to be
much alternative to getting close to your partner,
by which you understand her need is not antiphonal.
Her availability, you say, is like a line of credit:
It's only there if you promise not to take it down.
She appear to be perfecting the sex-free marriage.
"I didn't know, is there a rutting clause in the marriage contract?"
"Although our under things share the same hamper,"
you say, "our bodies share no intercourse."
You don't have free run of de sanction pits;
you invite her to admit the inadmissable, that finally
even from a topic after dinner this recede.

"As Mildred Watchyourbloodyaim and Harold Offbyayard,
you must agree, we the longest-running absence on TV."
"Agree," she say. "You mean as in 'agree'?
You want to marry 30 seconds at a time," she say.
She call you a libido in a three-piece suit. She ask
why she must go through and you must go through dis grimace of ecstasy.
She say you remind her of an artesian well.
She say it supposed to be a pleasure for both
but you come on like de Normandy Invasion.
Like The Return of the Blue Hoax. Like a one-man wrecking crew.
Like substance abuse. Like a hamper of Benzedrine.
She say you regard her as a kind of libido caviar.
"Dat would be an interesting principle of trade," you say.
You observe dat de husband have despositary rights,
and she to be available for purposes of loin-shudder.
"And if I'm oversexed," you say, "you're neversexed."
Quite the misanthrope, she take an aphorist's approach.
"All you want," she say, "is to do weird crittering.
Like a bladder you pursue a trapping and holding strategy."
She ask if you know the process isn't supposed to draw blood.
You want her to be your Barbie enthwacko, but she draw the line
when you want to carry her around on a cookie sheet.
She give you 15 yards for holding and illegal procedure.
You say she walk around like a literal interpretation
while you, you merely taking liberties wid de text.
She's welcome, you say, to scream and bell-weather bitch as she wish
but sometime since, she quit the business of allure.
"Flannel nighties, sweat socks, great appliqués
of priggish cold cream, dese are strategies
to keep a goombah called your husband at a goodly bay."
To which she give "Nothing of the kind" in reply.
She instruct you on your ineptitudes,
de foibled inadequacies you bring to wedlock. What you seek

is comfort and access aplenty for your fizzled wick.
But you got all the stamina of a shrunk dick. You go off
like a party popper, all small surprise and little consequence.
Her friends say, "He *looks* like he would have a small penis."
"Well I, for one," you say, "am glad my genitalia
are externalized." "More to show, less to tell."
How you have sex remind her of how you eat breath chips:
you enjoy it but it put your partner through hell.
"And *you*, after eating smoked oysters, have petrochemical breath.
But you a hard woman. You must have left
your sex on de White Sands Proving Grounds."
You wonder what she been adding to her cereal
dat turn her into Stone Woman. "Welcome to Ulan Bator,"
she say. "And you can forget the pink perfunctories."
"There you go again," you say, "fostering family values."
You bespeak her truculent *costanza*, her colnate *tomney*.
She hasn't had a chance to get mad about it yet,
but she ask if dis is part of a larger pattern
of embarrassment. Quite full of *Thus and so*,
she give you a speech close-captioned for de hard of hearing.
De ideal companion you never did become;
rather you become maddening in more subtle ways.
She declare you unfit to eat Braunschweiger,
to shovel frost on Planet X. You say
her conversation be a chorus of learned responses.
She a woman who wear her trousers like a veiled threat.
She use a metaphor for coupling to describe her opinion on dat.
She suggest you must have shrink wrap around your head.
"No need," you say, "to be convivial to de point of pain.
But why have you trained the dog to pee on *my* side of the bed?"
"You do whatever your glands impel you to do," she say.
"Well Omni—onni—oni—on," you say. Now that we have entered
the goddammit phase of this relationship, you ask

why she take marriage as a right to be unreasonable,
why she give de fling of her head to everything you stand for.
And why, after marriage, her brief bloom has flared to fat.
You ask if she understand dat de female of de species
(in contrast to de hundredfold female of spiderdom)
is not supposed to be larger than the male?
She loathe and she attack. And, oh, she excoriate your soul.
Armed wid a compatibility stun-gun, she swing,
she hit you wid a biological haymaker.
You respond wid a French bread diatribe.
You say she roly-poly and no fun to screw.
She counter wid a slashing attack
and several verbal uppercuts: You so much ejecta.
You buy de wrong brand of apple juice.
De house is out of dental floss.
She want a divorce. To which you say,
"Dis marriage has been *routinized*.
You will hear from my attorneys,
Carley Marcuse Chutney & Copperthwaite."
"And you from mine," she say, "Neiderplatz & Codemerantz."
And you shoot back, "Trefoil & Tditten."
And she shoot back, "Sadukar & Kine."
And you, "Throckmorton & Bottommonger."
And she, "Hawkstein & In Vitro."
And you, "Erabus & Erabus."
And she, "Adonis & Horvath."
And you, "Buttshank and Poolridder."
And she, "Devastate & Honman."
And you, "Angst & Argh."
And she, "Gizzo & Sons."

Or maybe, instead, your spouse show a deep unsettlement.
It could be every mirror she come near
get worked out hard. Like a hunting rifle

she keep her body oiled. She long to use it.
In restaurants she show a thoughtful amount of cleavage.
Her valve a sort of valve to your money,
she go shopping wid her body. She visit
de cosmologist, de liposuctionologist.
Maybe she visit the dentist Thursdays, 5 to 5:05,
or the fire house, to help the boys practise the Fireman's Carry.
Maybe she take riding lessons from Ridley von Seven Eleven.
A stuffy winesocks from way back, he rumored to have
armies of wash pants, de world's finest collection.
A tall man wid back trouble, his spine resemble
a tennis racquet. He can only get erect, you hear,
when he face north. (Something to do wid lines of force.)
A woman he consider a natural interchange.
Like an oenophile he go in for vertical tastings.
When you call his house in search of your wife, his Butler say
"She servicing the Master's heliotrope." You call again, he say
"The Master bench-testing a girl named Salmonella."
When Ridley come to the phone, he apologize for his Butler:
"He my Beefeater. He fuck the girls before I do."
You go to his house on Party Sample Road.
Under his stable window you hear your wife:
"What you going to do, melt in my mouth?
Come on," she say, "revival time."
He warm up wid a little low-grade humor, comparing her
to the legendary Marmooth who take her men like rolled oats.
He want her to meet his cousin, Sealtest von Ypres.
She propose they all meet for an Ungaro Manoleté
at three o'clock in the afternoon. He ask her to take
the postilion position while he find good footing.
He dispense wid de formality of trousers.
She shed, not tears, but her underpants. Wid her legs
she put him in a Salamanca gridlock. He say he can't
get off in de back stirrups of a *Better Wait a Minute*.

"And dey call dis Nature's Way," she say.
And he, "Mind if I slip in here?"
"Is dis," she say, "why they call you Monsieur Quicksilver?
What happens," she say, "when you give it the full awry?"
She take his Walcott and give it a haul. He respond
wid a grunt dat cause de horses to rear.
In despair you seek advice, you consult
a tract put out by de Ministry of Orgasm:
"How many men marry an ass?
How many women, a portfolio?
How long for a look pronounced by cosmetics
to boil off to the hard pudding below?
How can soul and smoke be mates?"
Your dreams of a torrid monogamy go up in a flum of flame.
All your thought is how to get out of a burning plane.

    At dis point you look back and you may see,
between de sexually unsuccessful marriage
and de sexually unsuccessful singlehood,
dere is de No-Man's Land of promiscuity.
You enroll in de Catchascatchcan School of mating.
You run a "Personal" in de *Bathsheba Bar Encounter:*
"Adam, 31, from de Guinness Book, seek Eve
for companionship leading to major event of de nerves.
Don't write unless you love music, art, good talk
and have big breasts. Must be able to skip rope."
Suppose a girl approach you on de street.
Something about her say inveigle.
She wear onomatopoeic duds, sizes too tight.
In a short skirt, wid an engaging reveal of thigh,
she dressed for Oorachie. In a mactatable ormolu
she walk de *feelie endwindle,* de *ruttable enfraisne.*
She got de hologram hair in a fracas cut.

What's more, she got tag-team mammaries,
big scoreboards, federally-insured *shamangas*.
She of a seismic pulchritude. Wid de bold address
of large-lashed eyes, she say "Dey call me Sugar Bush."
She say "Dis be your week to scallywag.
You a sausage on my hit parade."
You say you neither teetotal nor titillate.
She propose a sweaty pact. You two will do
everything allowed by legal eye contact.
She will introduce you to fluid dynamics.
You will have de freedom of her, to do
what you will wid your exploratory probe.
She will raise de Romeo flag, which mean *Come on in.*
She will be willing to éverte her havarté.
"You will be," she say, "a transubstantiated boy."
Wid an "Es que vous et Ready? Es que vous et Set?"
she offer de Polar Plummet, done wid no visible means of support.
She offer de Grand Gongol, de Compleat Engulfo,
after which milk and cookies will be served and naps will pertain.
If de gentleman will present himself like a candied yam,
she will give him a deluxe metempsychosis.
Off de side cushion and into a corner pocket
she will try de Matchapee Be Careful.
If de gentleman will place himself as far forward
and as low down as conditions allow
she will attempt a Zousner Overflight.
Dis will be like a Herdunsey Overflight
but wid flaps up and bomb doors closed.
Dis will not be "Thirty Seconds Over Tokyo,"
not "Sixty Minutes." Dis will be "Ten Days Dat Shook de World."
After, sorbet will be served to clear the palate.
Den she will introduce you to de dreaded Krakatoa,
for which you must be 21; followed by

a Zircotti Thumb-Down, which involve elation
and a Tallywhacker Override.
"Dis will be," she say, "an Actifed workout.
It will leave you weak-kneed and kidney-stoned.
At the end you will wonder why your brain is still alive."
She invite you to membership in de Sexual Pioneers.
Perhaps you'll try the Sybaritic Two-Step, the 'Parmicetti Hoe-Down.
Perhaps you will try a little of de Weimar Why Not,
the Siegfried Stomp, the Degradation Polka. She will play
the Taken Wyandotte and you, the Hessian Tractor.
"No need," she say, "to be a slave to your assumptions."
She cock de purgatory of her butt, she show
ever so slight of crack, she hint at de Burgess Elimination.
By creative misuse of your bodies' parts you will proceed;
by creative mismatch of his salients,
her apertures; and hers, and his.
For ten dollars more of ecstasy she will do
some additional sin. She don't preclude
de San Jacinto Holdaway, done wid a single hand;
de Ballwalker Countdown & Ballwalker Amplitude,
for which de pants should be uncomfortably tight.
Even the Ford Elbow Dance, characterized
by brutal shifts; which include a three-day grapple walk
and for which groin protection is required.
Her price list is according to the orifice,
wid due regard for wear and tear.
Come visit her on her bed of broken jambs
and she will offer you a discount on account of Lupercal.
If you feel the broad hanker, if you gonna lark
the honeymount, gonna put her in the loinhold,
then soon enough she will lower her moist,
exactly matched proclivity onto your
intensely interested protuberance.

"Come play my ditherqualm," she say,
"and I will enfold you in my great loose Henry.
I will be your vanishing act to the inward universe."

Too good to be allowed, you go wid her.
"Have you ever," she say, "strolled the stews of Potsdam,
ever stalked the upper stews of Sectionville,
Yerba, and the arc of de Arctic Circle?"
Swinging her purse, she recall conventions and tricks
she's known: The Tibetan Prayer Wheel, the Cake Walk,
the Artilleryman's Salute (for which you need butter, rope, a tire).
She discuss the importance of proper breathing.
She recall each declivity,
wid its own school of depravity. By all means,
she will want to introduce you to her friends.
("Dis is Madam Percale, who keep our time sheets.
And dis is Agnes de Millheart, who offer affordable access,
and Buppy de O'Heart, who does not. Meet Miss Demeanors,
spokesperson for Panty Pride, and de Gustibus Cheerleader
(hers is a corrupt pageant of beauty).
Meet Lowell, Mass. (her middle name is ,) and Helptippee Unload,
who believe dat every tub should stand on its own bottom.
Dis is Jeopardy Coterminus, who show herself
to be plug compatible. And dis is Chère Libido,
who wander around de park widout restraints.
Dis is salubrious Alice and dis lugubrious Sal.
Meet Mucho, who is cute if not beautiful,
and Celeste Hawkspittle, whose thin, forbearing look
(we call her Bolt Upright) is irresistible
to clients like Jeroboam Boumedienne, who are failed dieters.
Dis is Sandy Wasteland, an acquired ebvotic taste,
and Chastity au Swell, who have some moves she going to franchise.
Meet Hospice Colenecose. And her sister, Hospice.

And dis is Cindy. As in Incindiary.
And here—whose name fit her so well I can't remember it—
is a garden of anatomical delights.
Meet Lotus Curve—she of de heightened eyes and wide,
expectant look—who hail from de Kingdom of Eye Shadow.
(We call her de Egyptian Furrow.)
Meet Zia Zion, de Black Maria of Wilson Street.
Say Hi to Alarmie Kinkadoe, recipient of
the Dufresne Dumpney Award for extravagant underwear.
(She will play you a round of Far Bloomers.)
Here's Eve Pusillanimous, who do de E Pluribus Unum.
And Tekamaki Tum Tum, who have a migratory belly button.
Meet 'tove Enlargely, who sport ecktuberant enselmos,
and Pudenda Avocado of de elongated Ungaro.
(We call her Wholenose Parking.)
Meet "Cheeks" Almighty and her sister, "Tits."
(I bet you didn't know dat breasts dat size exist.
Dey were featured as protagonists in a underground movie.)
Meet Ballwalk Le Bertle—at de nooky bell she go to work,
and Linda Tantalus, a Kamikaze Change Artist.
I'd like you to meet Certain Stitch, who like
their jockey shorts to fit her men like tea cozies.
Dis is Mary Belesheim Boatlicker,
here from Iowa to visit her sister. And Ventana,
whom you can fold and unfold like a dollar bill.
(What she offer is enacted submission.)
Meet Mega Byte, who will do it for table stakes,
and Humidity O'Buff. (Hereabouts she known
as a whereabouts. Ignoble cooze, she permit double parking.)
Dis Alacrity Atlatl, who can do de alleyoop complete.
Meet Hospice Yum Yum, who measure success by her effect
on her man's coefficient of expansion.
And dis is Obeurrahaut Modigliani, whom you will want

to know if yours be a pistol for a different grip.
She will don constable clothes and a Broadmoor stimulator.
She will perform *achtung* on your ebullient cannister.
Dis is Nel Mezzodel who, blindfold,
can recognize an orifice from its signature scent.
Dis is Lammakamma Ding Dong, who fall in love
at every turn, and Dageurreotype von Sleaze.
Meet Multiple No No, who have a strong, ongoing interest
in the opposite sex, and Ingres de Angre, who have a strong,
ongoing interest in the opposite of sex.
Dis is Philately Corso, whose fingers understand
what's underneath the other's skirt, who is
de Variorum Edition of her persuasion.
Dis de once-torrid Rotunda Peenemunde
(so hirsute in de forearms and de go-between),
now known as Aged Llewana; and Ancient Ravioli,
who knew Napoleon when he was little. Have I missed anyone?
Dese girls, all, are fun-loving and herpes-free.
We will have uproarious times.
Dey will jack you off in a paper cup.")

    You ask how she come to be in this line of work.
"We come dis way by decrements," she say.
"Would you believe, I was de Pippi Longstocking of my day?
Den Fantasy Manager for de Buffalo Bills.
We start out young, beautiful and dirty.
In the end we just dirty. Someday
I'll walk around like a libido leftover.
Old Hatch, dey'll say, you make love like a vat.
Someday I'll be a depopulated hag,
dried like a root, unused as a storm drain,
the basement of a house long ago burned, filled in, gone feral.
But I think it's a great profession, *if* you can enjoy it."

You come to her hotel, which have a somewhat temporary look.
She ask for your trousers and she leave the room.
She don't come back. You find dat your wallet,
wid its reduce of bills, has gone de way of all flesh.

IV. The Death of
the Appreciator

Y ESTERDAY, YOU SEE dat man
       and de piecemeal sequence of his return?
Dat be Épergne de Hogney, de state Appreciator.
His job be to marvel publicly at Grace,
to action in de people's minds
what de assets of de Kingdom can become.
He stand in a field of goldenrod and point
to an incompleted post or so:

"Gonna be the Hotel Incontinental
(built on the ruins of l'Hotel Inconsequential).
500 rooms, and I prophesy No Vagrancy.
Every room will have two candles and a Bible.
De guests will arrive by Packard convertible phaeton.
Everything will proceed by signature, the Hotel
will cater to those who find it boring to be good."
He slap a pile of iron ore: "Gonna be
a 60-kilo fine steel wheel, rustless and true.
Gonna be trucks on a Class One carriage. Gonna turn
like happy click-click wheels of commerce
on de Federal Ferro Carril.
Gonna bring próduce down from the Frontier.
Gonna bring down the national debt."
He a man of letters. He make dem round and high.
Quite neat. He a factory for de well-turned phrase.

       He found to be appreciating the undercarriage
of one of de Overruth girls, a Bedlam Sans Merci
name of Luxury O'Twee. Luxury,
of de famous lap: When she introduce her huge
besoin in de neighborhood, grown men take cover.
Who know, maybe she tottle by all tits and hips,
in a capstan gown or michaeled halter.
Who know, maybe his proudflesh rise and point
like a crude homing device.
Maybe she give him de What-Are-You-After? stare
and he catch a whiff of impropriety.
Maybe she pleased by the undeniable "affair"
of dis affair. Maybe dey match dere mouthal parts.
Who know, maybe dey nibble de nuptials.
When she see the size of his intent, perhaps
she decide to give his case a frank handling,

to play moon maid to his Tuscany erect.
Perhaps she bare her eenie meenies, her sizeable
shenanigans and offer him a slice of thunder pie.
Maybe she touch him on de feel-good.
Perhaps he tickle her in de snickly abode
until she Sakajaweha. Maybe she hold him
by de long-neck until he Eniwetok.
Perhaps he prevail on her to practise-propagate,
to mock mate. He will take de pole position
while she assume de position for replenishment.
But in the moment of meet, of all that is She and what is He,
maybe he come on like a marital aid
dat get worked only for its own sake.
He address her savory wid immaculate care,
perhaps, den dispatch her wid a sudden shove.
Maybe in his view, she there with her inclined pivots
and adjustable nodes simply to porter his load,
but she think there should be something in it for her.
Maybe he think she want to be his demi-dunno,
the object of his *semen componens,* dat she want
to do de tev and stomp, de rubber Whitney.
Perhaps he have a specialized sense of humor; he think
she like to be beaten and changed into pants on Thursdays.
Maybe he specialize in beastly behavior, he drool,
and she give de Cochise refusal, wid a harrumph of hair.
Maybe he come on like insect life, like a Lebanese compost heap
and she, in a high-dudgeon snap, give him de *ego som popere:*
"You think I like a finger grope followed by a one-up?
You must think I was born in a Vulcan cane break.
Think I was built to be a lactating ewe?"
Or maybe she say, as quiet as a polyp drop
on a dissecting slab, she take a dim view of his proceedings.

De Appreciator amiable his Querriers.
He samovar his hosts. He insist dat dey go first.
He admire de spit shine and de press of his detainers' duds.
He feed de meter of dere mutter.
He commend de vigor of dere regard but
he sound de bell-note of incredulity.
He surprised at de heads-up nature of dis Inquiry.
He suppose de Justice boys must do dere job.
He assure his Querriers he bear no ill.
He wish dat justice to its full extent be brought.
Speedy justice is de way, he wish a "speedy and complete" —
and of course acquittal to a fare-thee-well.
He wag de likely outcome. He pretty soon his severance.
He prophesy a laugh come dis p.m.
He pshaw, he pooh-pooh, he besmirk de rumor of a gaffe.
He shoo de rumor of Marquandish wrath.
He unforgettable de Marquand's oaths.
He deplore dis as a palsy gone to pageant,
dat such misunderstanding could erupt.
He declare de misadventure a pack of nouns.
He monstrosity de complete affair.
Dis no landfall for his detractors,
dose prophets of contempt, believe you me.
Global fellows such as we will understand
dat a misunderstanding is de understanding of a Miss.
Dis a felony dey could all relate to.
He suggest dat His will soon be Hers.

And now the deadbolt man, Lafarge Lafui, read the findings:
"Huizinga Huizinga, the *nada* man, the *jamais* man,
beyond the liberties of tense the *ex post facto* man,
is most pleased to announce Épergne de Hogney
has been found guilty of capital crimes:

false prophesy, and worse, false gaiety,
and worst, for trying to live a fantasy.
For these infarctions and various penile infractions
he shall pay the painful pittance. He shall be reformed.
Let him take a lesson from de Dancing Master.
Let him learn the architecture of olé.
Let him, finally, gain stature from this experience.
Lafarge Lafui, Master of Revels   Regrets Only   Casual Dress"
To which de Hogney make reply:
"I never touch de lady's noble valve.
I never touch her upper stave.
Nor paps nor privities,
I touch no part of her hierarchies.
What I admired was her noble verve."

    And now, to witness the Punishment:
Comes Wilmoth the Outré, stiff Progenitor,
Comes Milords Tenfly and Tengumbo,
Comes the Brothers Conduct, Lewd and Lascivious,
Comes a whole Hoboken version of gentry
reptilian in a crust of jewels, followed by
the Butterfat Boy in his invented notions of finery.

    And now, *harup harup o'dee*, dey march de Hogney
to a showing of the instruments: the Voter's Booth,
where citizens are packed in ice to preserve dere liberties;
Smote Stones, for juicing his posterity;
The Shopper's Maul; the Citizen's Arrest;
the Pest ("Your Name Here") Control.
On the spot, Épergne renounce renown.
He rectify de hubris, he recuse
de rancid palsey of his earlier proclaims.
Come to think of it, he do recall.

He palpable his regret,
he disavow de vixen heresy.
And now de Chief Querrier, a tourniquet
de name of Mangle Surcease, an orotund
noncom with traces of hysteria,
an afro wid vociferous hair, assume control.
Épergne commend Surcease for de fashion statement
de scalps make, hanging from his belt.
"And dreadlocks are wonderful, turning your head
into a mess of telephone wires like that."
"Welcome to the Wrecker's Ball," de Querrier begin.
"For political prisoners we have a little extra, a little special."
A master of relaxed intimidation, Mangle explain,
"The unexamined life is not worth living.
And the capacity of a being to produce locomotion
is a sign of its perfection. So say Aristotle."
"Are you going to hurt me?" "Only if you're good.
We going to perform elective surgery on you.
First we subject you to a roly-poly thumb screw.
Fingernails and toenails, dose little spatulas
of bonelike stuff, wid de help of pliers we withdraw.
Den we take de keystone out of de autocleft—
dis is torn in a livid string from out of you.
When your sciatic nerve begin to emerge
from your nostril, we know de pain to be intense.
We'll watch what things you'll do to stay alive
that the body didn't know it was capable of.
Down you'll go until you barely
fit the definition of a man."
"Please don't torture me," de Hogney say,
and Surcease, "Oh, so you're an optimist."
"Hold on," de Hogney say. And he, "Hold still."
When dey hook de Hogney to the Dancing Master,

he muddy himself, he do a bladdersplat right on de ground.
As when the lift of a plane rolling at full intent
begin to capture the wheels from the runway
Touch... Go... Touch... Go... Go!
the 'Master's hairlifts wean Épergne from gravity.
He say *OK,* and then *Oh Yeah,*
and then *Oh No* and then just *O-O-O-O.*
He inaugurate a renaissance of pain;
wearing a cap of it he do uncustomary dances:
He do the Golliwog Cakewalk.
He trip the light Heraldic.
He do the tap dance *compris.*
("See how he dance with weird feet,
he dance like a Outrigger Boy!")
Totemic in the haul of gravity,
he pledge allegiance. He deeply regret.
He "Oh my God." He "I so sorry. I so stupid."
He confide the greatest secrets
he can imagine dey might like to hear.
He babble de hardscrabble of *Keep Me Whole.*
And all the while Hockstetter O'Dell and Offsides O'Twee
argue at a round of sildebordebellio.
And Galliacko Furness and Breckreef La Poste
maintain a languid palaver until Surcease
direct to take de Hogney down.
They kick him in the poursuivant.
They rack de balls. They chalk de cue.
They give his body *What For* wid a canvas hose,
which raise de impressive carbuncle.
(This they call Batting the Vertebrae Out of Bounds.)
Then they haul him to the Caterwaul,
the instrument that going to lend de Hogney stature
for the party of the second part.

Épergne gasp "You got de wrong man."
and Surcease answer "We got de wrung man."
Dey catch his digit in de mangle and take a turn.
Surcease ask "What are you learning from this?"
And hearing de reply he throw the switch to Tumble Dry.
Épergne falsetto innocence. He Irish tenor it.
He chanty his remorse. He Godzilla his despair.
He octave octaves. He trill de inmost folio.
He sing a literine contralto. And all the while
Malateste Ouvert and Moishe Hoolihan
play a scrabbly pinochle for his cape and shoes.
And all the while Mmsa Oopsa and Lama Sabachtani
sing *Olie Olie Sang Froid* at his feet.
And now they ease the tractors on Épergne,
the cuffs and collar, for his comfort.
Épergne cough up a crème brûlée;
the shape of him was slightly tarragoid.
But he bejabber thanks. He mumble the grace note of *OK.*
He make the constant sniffly aside. He hive de soul.
As the catchpiece ratchet like a gentle reminder
Surcease say, "Did you want to be liked
or did you want to make a difference?"
And hearing the reply he throw the switch to Spin Dry.
De 'Preciator's voice describe a labile curve
so forthcoming it could be ecstatic
over a main event of de soul. The timbers
of his body work like a ship's in heavy seas.
Brown and yellow cargos discharge from its holds.
They make a monster pew. On his hershey squirts
de boys make jokes of de bowel family.
Dey make of him an olfactory event.
They deride his dim confessions, his insistence on remorse.
They pettifog his mercy rides, his efforts to rename the day.

And now the Brownian motion of the Caterwaul
begin to lend Épergne de Hogney stature.
He reach new highs. He go to great lengths.
His grasp at last a good foot longer than his reach,
each of his apertures lengthen to an oval take on life.
In the seize of diphthong he leave behind the simple *O*
of vowels shucked of word pods, of consonant canisters.
As his experience surpass the reach of language
he communicate perfectly like a pig. He shuffle off
into animal *yuff*. He join the signal corps.
His language a linguistic pawing in the air,
he make de frantic sign: "I got de answer."
In lodgepole semaphore he *Mayday* his intent,
he make de frantic signal for relief.
To the fibric beating of his heart,
the *Just-A-Second* nature of his breathing,
the jerking of his limbs in a *Get-Out-Of-De-Way* way,
they commend him on the finest posture of his life.
They merry at his sockets popping like champagne corks.
They toast him wid a quart of Estonian aquavit.

    As the grosgrain of his musculature let go,
they pronounce him St. Elastic.
As de poor man grow by fits, by starts,
an older soldier point out to the younger's "Gee"
how de catastrophic salad of his body
resemble a chicken cleavered for a family of twelve.
And dis, I realize, be a moment of fellowship.
Sorewalk Suplupple, pickin' de pants out of his crack,
Sympathy Hose, eyes inapparent behind sunslants,
watch for the nacreous turnabout,
wait for the Carioca flutter.
They so attentive to his distress

because they know the manner of his dying
will be the signature of who he be.
And when his eyes begin to glitter
and he fever after death's cold compress;
when the end come up like a prevailing wind
and his soul like a mainsail fill and pull
as if to leave behind the body's boat,
as if wishing itself to sea,
dey hang Épergne de Hogney wid a sign:

UNHORSED BY HIS AVID SEED

And he hang in de wind. He slowly crust. He cure.

V. ECLOGUE OF AFTERS

I TRY DE ORGANIZED religion route.
You know de head prelate, Apotheosis Combe?
No starveling padre he, de portmanteau
of his belly precede him into de room.
A man of simple tastes and prodigious appetites,
he call de world a second helping of abundant broth.
To questions he reply "These be gustatory issues."
or "Curds and whey. Everything is curds and whey."
A nose like an upturned *Maybe*, he known as de hog pastor.

Each step a quake in all directions, wid three,
maybe four parts to his walk, he move
wid surpassing slowness under a parasol.
He wear a pair of enormous fan pants at de beach;
sunbathing, he require an acre of sun.
A man of violent size if he weren't so slow,
he move in a kind of episcopal restraining brace.
Hurryless, he walk the wide wale of his privacy.
He show a kind of planetary fatigue,
he live in a catafalque of shade.
Often he make provision for his mortality.
In his memory he place a plaque
inscribed "Placed in his Memory."

He lecture on japonica. "The rain roars!
Listen to it agrarian! Of the overlapping,
competing flora, each gets its. Leviathan oaks
above it all, the privet beneath it all,
down to fiddlehead ferns small enough
to know better. Even de inciteful ivy
and rhododendra long in de tooth.
But look at de un-unregenerate weeds,
de white pines' untended, candled growth,
de emasculate hemlocks. No wonder," he say,
"my faith in gardeners wavered and fell."

Prelate Combe, he smell of discount fragrances.
He speak in *double entendre* to de Congregation:
"Will all the men please get a grip on themselves."
"Will all the male members please stand up." Like dat.
In the confessional he write down addresses,
he emerge from fifteen minutes of reaffirming snooze.
His chorus sing wid an unconventional dissonance.
He known to beat a stern measure, to take

de choir boys by octaves, to reach for dere high *C.*
He *Of Course* to dere request for private voice.
Dey say he cite much holy scripture for épreuve
de unfit hole will do just fine for a man in his condition.
He enter the swollen hold of his consistory
wid a look common to men wid overheated testicles.
He emerge a somber and fresh xenomorph.

    For him de architecture of de *sous* seem incidental.
"Lust, if dat is de name for de attraction necessary
for procreation, is mindless and derefore innocent.
Would you change de mating habits of de magpie?"
But he counsel de young men against too much of de
   hairy snapdragon.
"I speak of the magnetic entrainment of de prohibited."
With seminal intent he condemn immoderate desire:
"For what has the rutting of pigs to do with this?"
He lambast de smell of humidity and buff
as "part of de business of de barnyard."
"Imagine how lobsters grapple to reproduce. All
exoskeleton and compound eye, dey couple and insert.
Imagine, den, de intensity of de stillness dat ensue.
Dat is how we appear to de Creator."
He deplore de *sigh sigh* of denimed thighs:
"For *slovenly dictu,* dese be known cuntities."

    He lecture, in *The Responsibilities of Bliss,*
on the politics of joy. In his sermon
Who's Minding the Bastille? he discuss
the uses of ammonia for crowd control, he preach
the need for an appealing authority figure
who can lay claim to major amounts of respect.
Expert in de half-a-loaf, he praise
de sanctity of ownership, de purity of power.

We are in the Book of *Correlations*: "In the beginning
was the Void, like a turn-down of nothingness."
In that pre-dream of Creation, at the drickle of been,
all things equally plausible, the Maker see:
If creativity is the control of chaos through expression,
then Creation could abridge inchoate Chaos itself.
In a black blink He give the Word: And the whole Void flood
with the hot thought of light. In breams of brightness
daylight post its going, its coming—in scenes
for which Bach might have writ the background score.
In the gravity outlay that follow, He sort through
great swirling masses of alliterate star matter.
A notorious perfectionist, He go through
art gum erasers at a prodigious rate.
The sun He move around like a flood lamp—such heat
and aspiration coming from a dime-sized portion of de sky!
The moon He try like a depleting ball.
But then He look back, He sense He miss a ball
of substance, a world of consequence: one to carry,
holing the emptiness around the sun,
a burden of verdance through a temp of time,
a planet in its heat and heart. This earth,
the apple of His eye, He give His planetary indulgence.
"If We trick the skin and find such alluvials,
think what lie below. Could be nothing.
Could be a wonder. Could be miles of neural bore."
In hot and cold raiment—buckracious cloud-cover,
breaking channels of wind-river cloud—He clothe it.
Wid adhesive water He paint it, He make a water ball.
But unearthly seas He do not see as the sum of things:
"I see strokes of reef, like brush strokes of incompletion.

I see good growing latitudes gone to waste.
Let there be marked volcanics. Let islands of igneous intrusion
rise in the surge, a cave at a time. Let there be
whole continents of boreal intent. And now,"
He say, "let the rest flow in *Anent, Adroit, Ajoint.*"
Wid fructifying rain He borneo the land.
In the complete fragrance of the original earth,
hand over hand for light, the whitest green break through.
Black boughs put on green flesh. Mushrooms, almost meat,
almost speak. Grubs, all maw, bore the loam's abundance.
The size of hands, birds populate the hills.
The land He make to be loud wid bird bluster,
the plural voice of de island thrush. Recumbent kine
He make to rest dere wrinkled butts in meadow grass.
He notice the moon, how its light transliterate the sun's.
He try it in evening, but the stars dim in its government.
He try it in morning, but the blue of astronauts show through.
Unable to decide, He try it from time to time.
At this, the sixth instanter of Creation, He rest His case.
It was risky. It was successful. How *could* He but be pleased?
And He partake of the deep rest that Sunday enjowls.

Den come a kind dat was a soul blip before it was
anything else. To his Adam, to his Eve
de Maker say, "All but mortal created I you.
On you alone I do not hide My hand,
I place My signature. I make you, man alive,
to walk in the mild, mistral summer, to walk out
onto a *hollihan* of dew, to be the first to come
to trout-infested creeks, squirrel-spavined woods.
I make you to go to high country in order to go
to higher country, in search of mountains' snowy occlusions.
In the flood of enfilial twilight, in the soft embryonic air

to sit and watch the sunset *oriflamme.*
Look. In broadhead dielight the raptor sail.
Listen. In de seas off Grace, whale sing to whale.
Contemplate the lasting image I have worked
on the near side of the moon, foreshadowing you.
Study the way each oak reach up into the dark
of what it isn't. Let the world be changed
under the glacial ice of your mind, its prevailing winds.
Bring me news of the patter of rain on Tennessee long leaf,
of the Archimedes frog the set of whose jaw is not
to be beheld elsewhere in the phylum.
Spiders in the cold, bees in inarticulate
bunches hang from a day's work.
All in the eggshell of the new world
they wait for their names, to see what they will be."
To each, wid its glimmering *int* of possibility,
Adam, practically halt wid de hypothesis,
wid de faith of it and the risk, speak.
"Crow," he say to a bitumen bird in a crotch of oak.
Liar Liar Liar come a cawcaphony in reply.
"Heron?" he say to a bird like a one-eyed hunch. "Hawk,"
he say to one gone high on soaring incirculars.
"Salmon," he say to one bright with the thought of spawning.
"Hummingbird" to one mining the nectar of a large implant.
To a moving penumbra of needles he say "Porcupine."
To a nimbus of fir, "Squirrel. With your wonderful feel
for unsound wood, go fly the high oaks in a aviary way."
"Gerbils, aren't you?" he say to busy little drastics.
"And an exceptional, sensational species you will be."
"Tortoise," he say to one whose canopy have
de transubstantiality of honey poured in oil.
"*Crocuta crocuta,*" he say to one wid wrestler's shoulders,
puppy's behind, and orthodontic bite.

The animal pant and wait wid a pained grin. (Adam,
wid a sideways look at his Maker, correct himself.
"Hyena," he say. "Your parts only appear mismatched.")

Naming by indirection now, Adam say
to the multitude "Each in turn and all in good time."
Here was the flower as silken blade, oaten sentiment.
And here the dromedary of a single hump;
the rare short-waisted stockstill;
the emblem of the swivet and of the spee.
To the spider, whose poison gland is bigger
than his brain, he say "Best not to expect too much."
To the expectorated clam, "Better you than me."
To the tube worm living like a stovepipe off
de flum of flume dat come from de planet's heart,
"Good luck coming of age in de Marianas Trench."
"Cricket," he say to one wid legs vastly overqualified,
and "Honey Bee" to the insulphated honey fly.
"Shoo fly," he say to an arrowing
opposed to nothing in particular,
"go and iridesce wid irreality."

Now come a beast, garden-fresh,
evolved from quite a different premise.
"So how are we doing today?" say the Serpent to Eve.
"What a morning! Sunbullient, senpenitent,
air washed like a testament by rain.
See how the sun through the hemlocks push his warm
embodiment. Humidity has lifted. Grass is mowed.
Happiness, from a day like this,
is inseparable as a cow from its cud.
Yessir, dis Eden be de place for basking and creation.
For this is Heaven! (Not the rather antiseptic heaven

of the Wesleyans, you know, but Heaven
with a rainbow and a gayety of cumulus!)
Yessir, going to be a hot and limitless day.
Makes you want to be that something
under the clean-cut shadow of a cloud
that looks up, glad of shade. A day half-decent,
not half-bad. About 90% fine.
(Unless like me you miss the nobby and bupp of humidity.)
My trouble is, when I sit down to another day
of unbefuddled, agitation-free content,
I say 'De sundial's slow. Needs to be wound.'
Reclined in banks of unflowering Toldmenot
I think, 'Time to force de hydrangeas.'
'Is dat a bank of Impatiens over dere?' I ask.
'No,' say I. 'Intemperance! Impertinence!'
Oh what does a blind man do for buff!
Out on my gambols and arroves I hear
de *bapple* of a fountain, *bapple* of a brook,
and I miss whole days of rain.
I look at dose cirrus laid like tread marks to de future
and I say 'Is de weather with its foreknowledge
doing anything we should know about?'
I listen to birds in de bushes, full of bluster,
to bees at maximum innuendo, and I say
'This Eden be a book of a single page.'

    "Sometimes it's so hard to figure out which way
is up. Is a grape a fruit or vegetable?
What's the difference? Does it matter?
Is it 'Highland Fling' or 'Highland Flung'? And why
are all Cowboy songs written in de same key?
Woodwinds blow, brasses blow. So why is there no
instrument of the orchestra based on sucking?

Why does His variety lead to such disparity?
Does *disparity* enjoy the same root as *despair?*
Why does *enthralling* rhyme with *appalling?*
What about *prudent, puerile* and *prurient?*
Deprived and *depraved? Declivity* and *depravity?*
Cosmologist and *cosmetologist?*
Is *salvation* not a corruption of *salivation?*
Immortality and *immorality:*
Can it be, what separates these words
is no more than the difference of a *t?*
In the word *temptation,* how entirely
unnecessary is the letter *p!*
Or take testosterone: any word
with dat many *t*'s has got to be a mistake.
Why do *oversee* and *overhear*
enjoy such different connotations?
Why do we *strain* a muscle but *sprain* an ankle?
Surely *renal* deserves a better meaning than it has,
just as *vulgate* is a word that has not lived up to its potential.
(It *could* mean one who is both vulgar and profligate.)

    "None of it sounds very merry or very good to me.
Why are a person's *privates,* for example,
placed where dey are hardest to get at?
Why not relocate dem and call dem *publics?*
Is *pubics* an attempt at dis? And why do we
split up by sexes when going to the bathroom?
Simply because our body parts dangle differently?
Simply different ports and drainage points?
Why does the body dispose separately
of its liquid and solid waste? What's the difference
between cream and scum? They both rise to the surface....
I bring such questions to Him, but...too busy...testy.

He adopt dat highly-affected, slightly-perfected
look—dat complex irrectitude—of His.
Dis should not be over-intellected.
Your job be to keeper the covenant.
Now I know we not in a period of opinion generation.
I know we live in a jokeless time, but one could not
accuse Him of an indiscriminate need to please.
(Why must He call me 'that Livermore snake?'
To be prized but not praised: Is dat enough?)
His is a charismatic leadership, of course.
And of *course* He created the world, rare and powerful.
In this belief we live and move and have our punkle.
In a fable of photons, a Cambrian shell game He make it:
messy, chaotic, exuberant and, above all, loud.
But see how He sign it wid dat overriding signature
dat end in a scrawl of *You know what I mean.*
And see how He stand for a little extra applause?
In all of dis we see de use of mystique
to sell you something you don't need.

    "Now He an appealing authority figure. De best policeman
He can be. He have no bad habits, no addictions
except to power. In His prose He show it possible, however,
to be at once very important and very boring.
(He give you language, yes. But why? Unless, by littles,
to make you comply with the deep purpose of its course?)
He show up in the Garden, as irritated
as a copper beech dat's had its mulch disturbed.
Don't be adverse and curious.
Learn the forms if not what fills the forms.
('And You call Yourself an authority figure,' thinks I.)
He puff wid anger like a foogoo.
Ambition is not a commodity in short supply.

108

Stop acting like a go-between from air to earth.
But I find dis uncongenial. I say
each part of the Creation is a variable:
if it doesn't work, let's put a wrench on it and change it.
What if water *were* compressible?
And how would the world change if its freezing point
were varied, either way, by ten degrees?
(Do *you* think He look on His creation
as a smoldering pile of incompletion?) 'Use only the new,'
says I. 'Lacquer the rest and put out its eyes.'
Don't give Me *the Incorpuscular Sirrah*, says He.
What are you trying to be, a known quantity?
Well, verbal-di-do-da, says I to dat.
Who does He think I am, the toad of indifference?
Is this the day I must rehearse remorse?
I say bitching is good for the soul. You must
give controversy its chance. (Otherwise I'm left
wid dese reciprocals, protuberant and undispatched.)
A deific moniker is what I need,
one that outsized *ha's* could not contest.
I travel, very much, the safe side of Paradise
but next time around someone less God-insistent would be nice."

The Serpent, now on epiglottal cruise control,
explain the orrery enclackical,
the armiguess of guidensize. With quaternicus ease
the vocables run off his tongue. "Of course," he say,
"you can see all this through granite-colored glasses
and say *The principal sin is having a mind of your own.*
Then this garden be an opportunity, indeed,
to go to sleep. But dat's life in de breeding colony.
People are so incurably slow. They confuse easily.
Like animals: too stupid to be distracted.

Or you can have the temerity to be a thinker.
You can equal the sprung weight of a standing man.
If you have that restlessness a snake must feel
before it molt, then you would risk
religious entropy, some scattered apostasies.
Like an ice cube on a hot stove, you can have
a lively ride and maybe finish up as steam.
What you will find is unexpected,
like a rope of snails on a summer morning.

Maybe," he say to Eve, "you sing *Hi diddle diddle*
                                  I'm caught in the middle
                                  I don't know what to do."

He don't discount the chance of a beastly outcome
"but it doesn't get bad in ways you would expect."
It will be straightforward if not widout risk to find out.
Smarmy wid innuendo, he slide home the chickpea
of his Make Me, the *audace* of his prophesy:
"How could He but be pleased you would dare to know?
A javelin throw from here there is a tree,
a part of the beauty of that plummet place.
On that tree there is an apple
with the soft, severe flavor of afterlife."

And Eve, she go. And after, go to Adam.
She walk an original walk, in which the word
sashay would come to find its meaning.
She tell of the apple and the apple's presentation.
Wid de tip of her tongue she eulogize.
And Adam, he have de apple and he settle down.
The knowledge of what is good for you: It start up
like a thin note from the ozone— *O-O—*

it gather in the valley's hoves — *O-O-O* —
it helter like a wasatch *pon.* It wing,
like a transgression — *O-O-O-O* — to find a hosatch home.
"Adam," say Eve, "what is dat one large seed —
Is dat de single hanging fruit of a man in season?"
"Stand back," say Adam, "I don't know how long it's going to get."
She hold him tight. And he her. Until all the goodness gone.

About the middens of the middenday the Lord
return to the encharmèd garden of his enharmèd Eden.
Fresh from the fresh roast of Creation, He in a rugged mood.
Adam He say, as He roam the wide walks
like a spacking sparking thunderhead.
Adam He say, all thundery and tonneau, and Adam answer:
"Here am I, the imitative fallacy."
Wid His nose for imperfection the Maker say
You have the smell of death. Adam say, "Is dis
de first crack in de plate glass window of Paradise?"
and to Eve he say, "I'd like you to meet the Uppermost."
She tell of de apple and de apple's presentation,
how de Serpent effect a weaselly intrusion,
how he impart de wily seed.
Thank goodness you didn't land in the ovoid cotton patch,
the Maker say. *The knowledge residing in those boles*
you really *shouldn't have. But this the season for blunders.*
I leave you in my gardens of self-governance for a day
but, oh no, you couldn't be grateful for good weather
and an open window. Oh no. You must have
the hidden meaning of My world.
To Eve He say, *You champion a household lust.*
Dis just plain old, raw, unpronounced desire.
Like a Jeep tire after a blowout, the rubber shell of Eve
barely could hold the memory of herself, let alone air.

To Adam, *You follow a trail of invidio perfume.*
Like an Eritrean sand slide it will take you down.
Adam, he at a loss for words. He cry a free flow of tears.
Male and female, de Maker say. *I mean that separation*
to *have the integrity of an electric fence.*
But the two of you have made for a disgruntled planet.
Now, like a mendicant friar, take your bowl and sort it out.
Henceforth wander the world in piecemeal shoes.
Henceforth live without a shred of context.
I cede you a hassle-coded environment.
De woods will become decidedly deciduous.
Sit in the hunter's hole, swathed against low degrees,
and watch the interregnum yield light without heat,
sky without bird, woods without deer. Live lightly
on the land, a place of huts and abandonment.
What will you eat? Anything coagulate,
anything to reflate the belly's encumbrance.
Nuts one season, oysters another—
a chowder of clams, narrowly salty.
Here are a few simple rules: Whatever weather
you don't dress for, that is the weather you will get.
You will live in a dream of no natural enemies,
but you shall become an intimate of rend.
You shall know the pleasures of the bee sting.
You shall live in a din of nothingness, its arundel, its wan.
Nor will your soul rise like a suffuse to its calling.
Nominee Ondigne *I mean this to be a point of tears.*
From dis time on We start the clock. You may live so long
as the blue cyprus gives you under its limbs a room of shade.
When the time comes and the worm turns
(Already I see in you, with your blood unbungled
and your skin in scads, the shakes of aging.)
you shall know Me. Or not. Until then Mine shall be
a withheld presence. Go now to a world

as different as the architecture of Saturday from Sunday.
Go forth with My extreme prejudice.
To Me you're a couple of fronds in the park.
Slowly they head for the hills. As an afterthought the Lord say:
Language. I'll leave you that. To remind you
of the dominion you had— that's the consolation.
But the ersatz nature of its creation— that's the curse.
And one thing more, He say to Adam. *I'll make sure,*
whenever you are interested, Eve is not.

    Now what are we to make of dis charming myth?
In the hands of the storyteller, facts migrate...
and you nod off a lot. My charge require
a vividry of images and a modicum
of omniana. De challenge is not to bore you.
What do Adam and his apple have to tell us?
In God's plan dere was a place for Adam, who should have said
Happy to be here, happy to be part of His plan.
But no, he had a hunger: to eat de apple
of HAVING YOUR OWN OPINION OF WHAT'S GOOD FOR YOU.
Perhaps you think your life as boring and go-nowhere
as our low-down, state-owned radio station.
Daily you pray to Our Lady of Perpetual Acceleration,
but you fail to be caught in de swing and fest of history.
Perhaps you a man who never miss his three-squares,
his bean-wid-bacon omelette; a man who require
great quantiples of fatty food and, as a result,
feel like Man at his immotionary most.
Perhaps you have a physically gross disablement.
Suppose you a woman who have a problem wid facial hair,
a complexion dat look like a satellite photo
and skin dat could bind books. Your teeth are a mother lode
and your breath could remove paint. Yours appears to be
a life committed to uncompromising failure,

a shower and splash of insupportable debris.
Do not despair. De news is good.
In God's plan dere is a place for us each.
Like the authority of equipment—having a function and only that—
dere is an ideal form to your professional duties;
you sanctify your calling by living up to dat ideal.
If you an ant, be a very good ant.
If you wash cars, dat's what you amount to; be of good cheer
as you pass your day in de plumping and butting machine.
If you a dross dealer, deal in the dross
of auto bumpers and crisped tail-light lenses.
Frequent de scenes of accident.
Sweep up de palsied body parts of cars—
elbows of mufflers, thrown fan belts—
and, while you're at it, de latest dog fritters
and de irreverential containers of de fast food kingdom.
The butcher in his butcher shop retain
great hangs of meat to remind him of his mortality.
The baker at 4 a.m., he rise in a faith of clock.
He walk for miles to a powder of unmarked dough.
(Of de candlestick maker, enough said.)
If you an aquarium attendant, you stand in front
of de wall of incumbent water. You describe de fish.
As it be de brickmen's place to call out comments
to de noontide girls, so it be
de secretaries' place to ignore dem.
If you a plumber you deal wid toilets dat speak
like run-on sentences; you bring to bear
fifty years of flushing geometry. If you a shoeshine,
wid every stroke of de rag you give your secrets away.
If you a shoe salesman, inspecting old shoes,
you look at de failed footwear, you study it for size.
De poet, he lay a threadle of ink through a thousand pages;

his *Complete Works* he complete by jumping off bridges.
De Muzak man, he say "My job is to record
for elevators. I have hair in my nostrils, my ears, my notes.
The gift of my mediocrity is such
I can make any piece of music sound the same.
I can remove the sizzle from the steak,
the 'sound' from any group; I can make the finest songs
recognizable only as melodies.
If not a stand-up comedian, still
I'll be remembered as a standing joke."
De radio announcer, he say "Shrimp Ahoy!"
And for dat he collect a day's wages.
If you a newsman, deal with the news: "Folks,
today there was no news. Nonesoever.
We were hoping that the Bain sow would litter...."
If you a listener, you sort through the confusion of stations,
the babble of the world's fused frequencies.
If you a baseball pitcher, fast beyond the art of fast,
you put your life into every single pitch.
If you an advertising man, it's de same.
The accountant carry wid him exactitude:
In a wood case, velvet-lined, a meter bar
made by the Bureau of Standards for scientific use.
If you a lawyer, like a taxidermist you fix
the quivering events of life in stilled, vaulted forms.
If you a French teacher you teach the French *r,*
which is spoken like a lizard swallowing.
If you an English teacher you teach tense:
You got the perfect, the pluperfect, and the just-past perfect.
Then you got your forms of interjunction:
the indelicate interrogative, the peremptory imperative,
the explosive coercive and the rip-roaring expletive.
If you a scholar, your pithy *aperçus*

manage to be both apt *and* obscure.
If you a wise man, full of adenoid and talc,
you draw yourself to your full height up.
You tell us how it going to be. Full
of moral authority and exculpated fact
you are, for all your erudition and admonition,
merely a more articulated version of folly.
As purveyor of de future you never fail
to get it wrong. You a floppy-headed fool.
If, on the other hand, you a shaman
in the Northern Territories, you build a fire
and wave a blanket over it. In 14 days
dis will be a blizzard in New York.
In God's plan even the King have duties and a place.
He arrive by train: "We are here by virtue of de 3:59."
He move like the stream that splashes through property,
drawing after it the strings of ownership.
The job of his coinage be to carry his *emprunt*
like a resonance throughout the realm.
He, too, resent the tentaculars of wealth.
I've heard him say, "The most honest thing we can do is be honest."
(I've also heard him say, "As Monarch I survive
as more than tourist attraction. Am I so bad
as the Duke of Bergun would have you believe?
Even Bergerac au Bergerac would not accede to dis.

CONDITIONS
- An immediate return to monarchy.
- Full pardons for Cherchez Dior and Normande.
- A lifting of the ban on lime-green comic strips.
- An apology from the shirter for what he said about
  the undershorter (about *your* stock in *our* trade.)
- Whatever clothing can do for us, we accept.

We wait upon the day the Damrach constabulary say Enough.")
Even his dreams are not free of de cares of de crown:
"In the basement, down stone-flagged passages, to the reaches
of the emblemry...even now someone getting up
to put de finishing touches on my hamster sandwich,
somebody decanting juice from de long tall sallies in de 'fridge."

    Let me bring this to a shapely cumulative.
You seek a life as self-breeding as a sing-along.
But you have experiences and dese be shapitive.
You come to me like a nation of taxicabs;
wid de indiscriminate nature of horns you complain.
Like dogs to a postman you present a baying alternative.
I hear you say, "We a nation of fat jokes.
The Rich, the Famous, and the Flatulent."
You show concern for de unequal rights of patrons:
"A support system for poverty-stricken bluenoses."
Grace: "A nice place to live but I wouldn't want to visit."
Hunger: "A heartfelt throb they tell us to put behind."
Wid debilitated ohdarnits you say these things to me.
You're afraid of your own impatience so you come to me.
"Why can't it be like it always wasn't?" you say.
Cow-eyed and ophligettus you say, "Oh no,
I wouldn't begin to know what chances to take for dat."
Oh ye of little faith and less intelligence!
You think there's nobody on the other side
of the Confessor's screen? I am your Combe!
In matters of Church, I give you de Pompous Encyclical:
Labor is holy but ownership is dangerous.
In matters of State, I give you governing truisms
about which you will learn after it's over.
You read a book. Why put your mind at risk?

Books are consumables. Dey are combustibles.
Why follow Dewey on his march of decimal points?
De quibblers arrive: But what's good is not worth dying for.
The protester? He push cantankerous to a malign metaphysics.
A law-abiding renegade? No such thing.
Political unrest? Hard-boiled, de egg of state
craze and enfeacle de microbe populations
always trying for a way to get in.
Pretty soon, de goshawful smell of H_2S.
Anarchy be a subaltern *de facto* committee of one.
To forge forward in de holy hope of dynamite?
Dis how you dynamite de selfhood!
Rebellion be like an airplane crashing:
It kill somewhat withal de life within.
In my self-effacing capacity
as inspector of de people's spirit
(my public insignificance—I wear it
as a badge of honor), I deal wid all sorts
of de out-of-sorts. But you, as proper members
of your ill-balanced and ignorant generation,
are not trying to wander off de Inner Planet.
Lazy, insufficient folk such as you
are ruminants in search of succulents.
Like cars in a blizzard you are looking for someone to follow.
Lethargic, self-provisioning folk such as you
need guidance. You need to know what to know.
When first he beheld the endless, moderating sea
what filled the penitential Adam? I'll tell you what:
Respect. On earth as it is in heaven, Government mean
dere be one man in charge. Fealty: Dat's what's owed.
If the State is a hammer, then respond like a addle-headed brad.
Don't be a puckering fester in de body politic;
don't be the pestering antimetabole, either.

What is wanted is a great show of diligence.
Must productivity and pleasure vary inversely?
As you consider the linkage between carefulness and pay,
at the moment of emolument, consider this:
Sometimes all we can be is aftermath. Would you be
remembered as lazy opportunists or becalmed realists?
God give us a face wid 200 muscles so we can grin
and bear it. To be a good citizen: could dis not be
a comfort like the weight of covers on a winter night?
Oh maybe it is. And den again, maybe it is.

When I intercept him at de High Church holy doat, he say
"Special consideration we don't have time for here."
When I wish to share my numerous concerns
he say it doesn't matter. He doesn't care.
"What are you, the La Brea Tar Pit?
Encapsulate yourself, you idiot."
I tell how I ever so slightly detuned by de Regulator's bliss.
"That's the sort of thing you're not supposed to make plain.
That's *just* the sort of Mukden escapism for which
you could be justifiably detained.
For living within the rules," he say, "you get a living wage.
For living without, could be good, could be bad.
The world is full of people cutting their losses."
He tell me to assume my fair share of inertia.
"Undone by the day's funicular, be of small mind.
Let it arrest itself in small gridlockeries.
We are creatures of habit—as in using the phrase
Creatures of Habit. Be of the Diligentsia.
Be a little engine of need, engine of keep.
There is much to be said for faring. No flashling now,
you glitter wid inconspicuence.
A raggedly unimportant man,

you sparkle wid inconsequence.
Like a Japanese maple you do well in shade.
What you don't want to lose is the chance to be resultant.
The point is not to be right but to be alive."
He offer a pretty good explanation of certain consequences.
"Rules of Conduct help us to avoid
the need for Rules of Engagement.
Don't get yourself a bad name in a small world."

    I describe my life to date as de cocking of a hammer,
de loading of a bow. Time and again
I break through to the realities of my day,
but always the gun jump and miss, like a disrupted consequence.
I lack the ability to make things happen.
"Dere is a place for young men who, with great speed
and hebetude, want to make things happen.
But fix this in the shallow places of your mind:
A plane without power will—you may depend upon it—
find its way to the ground. If, like de red cardidinal,
you find it hard to be inspicuous,
find you lack de ability to zig and zog—
I find dis unavoidable good news.
Go back to sleep," he say. "It's the wrong century."

    I say "I going to leave my time, my kind,
my planet unaffected. I am dat prophet
widout no honor in my home. Like a Hooper biplane
in a backyard, I down to cowling and struts."
"Wonderful," he say. "Terrific.
A complete course in podiatry.
There is a moment, hearing a joke,

of standing outside it until you 'get' the punch line.
For some of us, dis moment may go on for years.
But is it exciting? It is *not* exciting
to stand here and listen to you listen to you.
So spare me the nits, the nats and the caveats.
It seems apparent and therefore unlikely that
you got no fears, no septorgonian mambas?
I advise you to ungunk your mind
of this urge from elsewhere to be relevant.
Try each of de positions of appearance. This will produce,
not action, but a comfortable state of mind.
You won't feel better, you'll just feel bad in a different way.
But you not going to make this easy, are you."

    "On de ship of life," I say, "seem to be somebody
down in de steering room, far aft of de bridge,
kneading de great gears in dere hands." Dis he probe
as deep as eruction, as a deep consequence of garlic.
From his teeth wid his tongue he dislump a piece of meat,
a piece of truly defected matter.
"This a slow night for great books."
On degree of difficulty he give this nine,
but within the fourth degree of consanguinity
he can make dis *mise en explication*:
"The clearest view of the oldest light in the universe
is not here. Go to a mountaintop in Chile.
Or check in at de Charkchothian Monastery.
When things of a riddle do not appear, check yourself
for hereditary emptyheadedness.
Trust the unresidual recesses of your mind.
If your angularity is irreproachable
ask, *What is de rule dat dese exceptions prove?*"

Spiritual knowledge, he explain, accumulate
de way dog hair precollect in ghost rolls round de floor.

   "The thing about the past," I say, "is how little trace
it leave of itself. And humans, not so much
as a fern print in Wyomingonian shale. Our fern prints
seem to be found on dose around us who survive.
Aren't we, finally, who our fellows say we are?"
The Prelate smile like a germinating seed: "The thing
about the past is that it's not a lot to have in common."
The Prelate smile like a yellowing periodical:
"The thing about the past is that it can't be changed.
We *are* more past than future, it is true, but mostly
we are present. Why should we carry within us the past
as present when the present belong to those present?"
Like a man who try to smile as he play de saxophone
he say, "It's very hard to live a life
that is relevant to later generations.
And an open question why one would want to.
Dat somebody hear of you later, what should you care?
But dis dey call immortality.
Think of all the dead that ever were,
how many the more chose simply not to be named.
As a diner have a concept called *Closed*,
sometimes the only good end is a dead end. Give thanks
that you live in a world that elicit a *Holy Cow* response."
A wisp of a smile visit the Petri dish of his face.
"The yearning for permanence, for life everlasting.
For this you may go wid my imparted blessing.
But a higher and a best use of your good?
It shall not be nor will it come to pass.
Dis not how it should be. But dis is how it is."

I try de organized religion route.
You know dat styptic assistant, Simone Behooverself?
No randy celibate, no corporate equivalent of a fat joke, he.
A man of medium footage, his tonsured head
move like a rim shot through the laity.
He chew hard like he mean it. No acceptor
of de light alcoholic compromise,
he drink his ale like a cold flush.
He imbibe it by de quaff.
After years of de angry cigarette,
his insides must be like a wall of smoked salmon.

On his Church he post a sign "No Floors in This Building."
Legend for his Sunday irreverence,
he tell how "There is a bomb in Gilead."
How Jesus to the daffydells command:
"Ready. Set. Burgeon."
In his sermon *Honk If You Love Jesus*
he say "Comes Christ on a ridden ray
for His incredible debut at Canaan."
He spend time lookin' for de Jesus trace.
Often he find it: Hog abortions are up;
by itself de lawnmower farted into life.
Salvation is "a roped soap, sought but seldom caught."
No pope on a rope himself, he run
considerably beyond most heresy.
The Bible he discuss ("The Bible? Yes,
dis be my Jesus cruller.") as anthology.
At de parchment breaks he as likely as not to say
"Is anybody else underwhelmed by this?"
"Sickness and Sin" he say. "Are these two merely joined
at the hip by assonance, or do they stand for sister things?"
He pattynoster wid a rum aside:

"What's de structural integrity of *dat*?"
De last words on the Cross, "Ohly Ohly Oxen Free,"
he cite wid "What's de percentage in *dat*?"
He say "Marty Luther's brother never got it right;
he insist on nailing 95 *feces* to the door at Wittenberg."
But one idea he have like a spike of intellect, a spoke
of his intelligence: he propose a priesthood
based not on celibracy but on abstinence from food.
("Only trouble, we lose dem in about 30 days.")
The sermons of others he etch wid an elegiac acid
("Are we playing jump-ball for Jesus?").
He give 'em de Anti-Christ
after which de collection is perfunctory.

    Parishioners he hunt wid a vanity carbine.
He telex the obese: CEASE
THE POTABLE INGEST STOP DIET OR DIE STOP
Not to be accused of wheedlery, he don't hold back,
even to Jean de Conflans, Sire de Damphierre:
CEASE SATAN OR FACE CONSEQUENCE STOP
A sandy sponsor of inveigh, he give dem
a full measure of de conscience smote.
In *Angers and Asides* he say "Besides,
think of what you will say on Judgement Day
when, like a lobster cooked and cashiered of shell,
like a tea bag in a wrack of boiling water,
you are asked to make a statement." But he speak, too,
of sensuality transformed to a craving for self-sacrifice,
of an ethical foundation and a combative instinct:
how these form the frame of a life beautiful.

ON BECOMING IN OUR OWN TURN VINTAGE

I am extremely pleased and demented to be here.
Gassed up and demystified I speak today
of matters of spirit, of impenetrable gloom.
Of the public man, the private man, the private man
within the private man. Of lives, how do we live?
Of life, what makes a good life good?

    In de great Ago, dere was
an emptiness of rocks like broken teeth.
Beside a geyser's soft, enpillared blow,
de percolating mud like aeons of fudge
go *Bilk. Ba'o. Bluk. What-O.*
Salamanders wid fins for inauspicious legs
let go heptapital gills; wid lungs for eyes,
wid spelunker personalities
dey grab hold the air a different way.
Fry of Ichthyosaur people Wyoming seas.
Amphibia skedaddle in imbricate surf.
The dun crawl forth, sexually mature, on the void to dry:
We having a planet-wide hatch.
Come a comet's *summit hummit dummit hummit:*
The dinosaur give a palaeontologic blink and was gone.
Come de Pleistocene *summit hummit dummit hummit:*
Odd-toed ungulates walk de earth;
come a homo-some-sapiens name o' man.

    From coelecantherytes to danderodes,
from de amoeba who think wid its shape,
down through the phylum *chordata inamorata,*
we know dat life is not particular as to de form it take.
What then are we to think of a species dat,

125

far more likely to sink than swim,
through the luckness of time prevail above all?
A kind whose eyes are wells of reptilian regard,
the throat a cave of winds, the skull a stone boat
bearing the Piltdown brain demanding and enamoring.
The hands—for all things gripped, an end—
the fine upstanding structure of the leg,
the watch-work knee on calf on ankle
on committed foot, balancing easily.
Consider the organ beds, what might be divined
from the lymph pools, the minimal salmon runs;
dirigible lungs; the red heart in its gristle web;
the stomach reducing ores of supper,
the interior mile of the blue intestine which emerge
to the damp partition of the 'gluts like a Klein bottle,
the inward universe become the outer.
Consider, if each part's part is so elaborated,
why the purpose of the whole is not.
And, until the animal itself elaborate
that end, whether any marvel has been made.

 White tail, he taught to flee dissent. Coyote,
to collapse on his prey. Right whale, to mouth his meadow's krill.
And Spider, to make one thing repeatedly.
(Out of his orifice, unheard-of muscles press
a cable mile, 8 hands pay out in junctions
dat he simply know. After the Maker's heart
he put the merest gloze on air. His hands take hold
of certain strands; he settle to see what come his way.)
Grackle, he croak, fluff, crap and glare.
Posting on reptilian feet, he sort through
the easy meat of the dim larval world.
And Worm, unless by dat bird decapitate,
or straightened on your fishhook's J,

he sculpt in the earth's long cowl
a hole continuous as history.
If a bear be so...ursine, a dinosaur so...saurian,
a monkey so...simian, is man's job not to be
human...whatever dat may be? To explore to the limits
what it is to be on this earth, out to de edges
of de human predicament to be what he can be?

Man: Is he a gravitometer?
Hygrometer? Inclinometer?
Or all of de above, an instrument
overpriced but highly sensitive?
Man's life: does it make a parabola
like the rambunctious bell curve of popcorn popping in a pan?
Or is it a long voyage on a rowing machine?
Up from the veldt, cheek meat uneaten overnight
by predators, how does man live,
dat his unused capacity for survival
not turn to ennui, atrophy, angst?
It be possible of course to spend your thinking life
on the dark central issues of the body.
What it does, what it wants to do:
the need to eat equals the need to excrete.
The harder quadratics of the need to love and to make love.
And those binomials, by no means easy,
of who and with whom. But suppose you decide from the start
to live on the higher grounds of humanism,
to shine with and express what it is to be man.
You ladle from the well of *Go*. You ladle and drink.
Taking care to take care, you put together
the apex and supports of a life
lived as a demonstration project.
In a series of easy but sequential steps
you follow the lodestone of Can, lodestar of May.

When you graduate from Calmmedown College,
de faculty and trustees ululate. Secretly
you are inducted into the "Butter and Hot Knife Society."
As 8 become 9, implying dere is a future and it is 10;
as headlights bore conical holes in the dark ahead,
your career proceed. Your résumé read:
"Pandemic trekker, scubist (cave, wreck and ice),
speed reader, deep listener, Layer on of Hands."
What then? sing Plato's ghost, What then?

You reach an age where you have delineated tastes.
Like a pair of collar stays you maintain appearances.
You speak wid a sensing nomenclature.
You are measured by your effect on others.
You rise to be Chairman of The Nothingness Society.
You found a Fellowship to honor drivers who have let
the other driver go ahead. (No one qualifies.)
You live by the empowerment of stairs,
the check of bannisters, the support of floors.
You preach the orderly existence of existence,
a world where idea and spirit inhere, congrue.
Your life, like the movement of a Swiss watch,
is all flutter and delicacy. You say,
"With or without the guiding hands of gods,
I do believe dat character determines fate."
You say your life is "in comport." Quite often
you address your heart: "How you doin' today?
You feelin' rested? You got 87 years to go."
Portable versions of you, your sons,
afflicted wid your maxims, become
your emissary seed, your name wraiths.
On winter nights you love to sit, mezmeronic,
and witness the extraordinary ritual of fire,

the subsumption of whatever wood is to whatever flame is.
You strike a match, give it time to get its grip.
You watch, in the black vacuity of de fire hole,
knobbed wid andirons, the coming of the consuming mastiff.
You watch de grow-lines of de fire become general,
birch in its paper *barl* foregoing into flame,
the wood burn merrily and well. Turned, the log
shows to the room its Dresden side. You love to look
at the glowing hold of coals in shapes that once were wood;
to poke them into a ruckus of sparks.
You tamp tobacco into the sleeping wood of your pipe.
Scratched, the match delays as if considering,
then catches to its next existence.
You draw down the lavender flame. The tobacco wakes,
not knowing if this is death or life.
What then? sing Plato's ghost, What then?

           Why then you age. You live to white-haired lengths.
Life you address wid an unrelenting openness,
a Fitzwickian acceptance, until the day
come for you to fork over your mortality.
You look in the mirror: Out of the distinguished face
of that silver-haired success stare the eyes of a fool.
Slowly your head forget its hold on hair.
Like the end of an ice age, your forehead's dome emerge.
You live in the context of your body.
You shovel food to the long belly,
the mouth bake the slow bread of its tongue,
the body accumulate against the day of hibernation.
The colon load and clear. Your body
and its pungent wastes become a dormant empire.
You join the set of the noticeably obese.
Your body an impressive *bub*, an aggravating

shake of pounds, people say *Hi. Your name must be Corpus.*
You enter the age of codgers. Of a sudden
the rest of your hair fall out. Followed by your testicles.
You walk in a shape of mildew. More and more
you live in the land of ago where friends —
everyone you've loved — has died.
Long a wakeful verbiage in the drawer
your memoirs, *Infarction on the Rappahannock,*
you make hagiographically correct.
("First, I'd like to say thanks for the chance to be
animate, rather than inanimate, clay. It certainly beats
weathering on a hillside for the past 80 years.")
You negotiate de final wording on your eulogy.
("In life he was known as de Retentive Ombudsman....")
Your Last Words planned (*At least I won't have to brush my teeth anymore.*)
you got everything covered but the future.
A retiree in a rusted-out car, you await
your supermarket wife, the pounding of
your economics stopped long ago.
You walk about, a dilapidated honorand,
like a landed airplane in search of a gate.
You tell the carnivorous jokes of the old: *I'm 94.*
I still have some hair and some teeth,
and alcohol still works its magic.
You join de ranks of de untoward and incapable.
Your life takes on the lost logic
of plumbing lines in old houses.
You grow to be a mannerism,
a mild scandal to your children.
When we go out driving, he has taken to riding in the trunk.
You come to the dinner table in a pork pie hat.
You still alive — pre-dead — but much of the day
you seem to dwell in de next abide.

Your job: to stand in a room and decompose.
Your mind swing like the needle of a confused compass.
As a finger service its nostril in a furtive picking
of de nose, you specialize in being oblivious.
One day, you catch de goshawful smell of oblivion.
Having cleared your *In Box* to your *Out Box*, you
for your next-to-last act place a pistol in de *In Box*.
What then? you hum the while. *What then?*

     As car owners bring to the body shop
their *Whoops* and *Christ Almighty* inadvertencies,
so, my souls, do you bring your lives to me.
To let the years go by in the slow routine
of simply staying alive under a hot sun:
it bring to man the animal the contént
of a lizard on a sun-warm rock. But it leave the soul
—the basilisk soul—unfed. Unrested. Unfulfilled.
A life so lived is like a meal dat has been reheated
in de same skillet for a week. Like a boat,
built to be buoyant, dat find its true bottom on a reef.
Whereto, the beautiful life of honor and fidelity,
if honor erodes to pride, love is revealed as self-love,
and pity, self-pity? And to what end? Dearly Beloved,
I am your Behooverself. I say to you,
live in the hope of doves, their sprightly white unkindledness,
the *Not Yet* of wings unflared by flight.
Live as if a person's worth
be measured by the reach of his care,
by gentleness and the curbing of desires.
Live by a clearness and acuteness of intellect,
by strength of will, by a love of order
and a high sense of duty. History shows us,
these are answers to the imperfection of reality.
These are cargos for the slow migration of the soul.

When I accost him at de High Church holy doat
he say "What are you, the Impenetrable Hedge?"
When I seek to share my numerous concerns
he say "What *are* you, a spectrographic analysis?"
I say "I feel like a man gone overboard,
trying to stay afloat by surface tension.
I feel like a millpede, feedin' on a turd.
Dem hundred legs, runnin' by de numbers,
wait for orders from de overcrowded brain
when — *BAM* — comes dis great foot down
on my unprotected protoplasmic head."
Slowly, reluctantly, he say "Yes, dat's not unright."
He allow dis was an oort cloud I could worry about.
But it's very important to be out of step.
Dere is much to be said for out of step.
On dis dere was a shared mucilage of understanding.
But to whom to address such bosky queries?
"Depend upon de throw-weight of de individual."
He mutter "I dislike hierarchy. I would minimize it.
But like the *Hindenburg* you must learn to cool down,
must learn to ride the stallions of compromise.
You must master your own catatonic fits,
not hunker down in a revetment of remorse."

I wonder at de meaning of my gassy purloins,
my squeamish suffocations. "Dere's no accounting for taste,"
he say, "but den dere's no accountability for it, either.
What we may have here is a deeper discount, a failure
to perform. As a gunslinger, waving a pistol
of horse caliber, would enter a saloon and say,

'What's de standard of perfection around here?'
so you a prisoner of old habits of intensity.
From the imperfections of Dodge, from a life by the campfire
singing ancient desperado songs, you show up like a brain-dead posse.
But if dat's de only pony missing in dis round up,
dat go under de category of weird but uninteresting."

I ask "Is truth-telling always an act
of self-destruction or self-congratulation?"
"Truth has become two-sided, the smooth coinage of realms,"
he say. "But what makes you think *you* know the unknowable truth,
the ungainly barnwash of untestable truth?
Taking the hindmost, the Devil say, is not the only path
to Hell—but I about to regret being here, aren't I."

"I thought I might have a chance to stand for something."
"Like detritus?" he say. "What are you,
The Predictable Onslaught? The Unhaulable Log?
The sun comes up, lighting this and that, but you cannot,
among the chairs and tables, find out from it how to live.
And the will to live a good life gains passion
from the knowledge of how close we are to living its opposite.
Of the Seven Deadlies, arrogance is worst.
What the gods hate most in men is arrogance of power.
Ditto for what men hate most in men. Each act
of unrequired generosity—or its opposite—
go into the great human canon. Or so you hope.
But as to how long you can draw on a life lived well?
Dat's a matter between you and your hairdresser.
The trick is to remain innocent but not naive.
If you can't be innocent, at least be decent."

I say, "At my end will I be able to say:
I was who I should have been.
I was where I should have been.
I was when I should have been."
"Talking to you is like talking to an organ transplant.
But here is my reply to dat.
If I were designing us I would shop the Kingdom
and, like the Meiji, take the best from each:
From the frog, hibernation in times of unemployment.
From the White Tail, infertility when there is not enough food
but a double drop of young when green returns.
From the oyster, the knack of changing sex
(if that does not dispel the mystery),
and the knack to work its bit of grit—any catch
in the comfort of its membranes—into an absence of pearl.
And after the fish of the sea and the fowl of the air
and every creeping thing that creepeth on the earth,
I would remove from our kind the knowledge of our death
so that like our German Shepherd, Nanny,
we take things a day at a time; we feel our age,
at most, an infinitely gentle retrograde."

"De mystery," I say, "is dat something happen and den something happen.
That a piece of clay stand up and sing, that in itself
impress the rest of us. That it lie down and shut up
impress us equally. What happens after, dat's de epoxy question."
De Prelate say "I am, I'm afraid, innocent of a lot of things.
But about my uncertainty I have complete certainty.
Life after life? De honest answer is,
we don't know what de Harvey Lichtenstein
on dat might be." His face do an involuntary cringle.
"But I could take de heavenside of dat.
I respect de gods as if dey were dere.

Hope against hope, I hope it so.
So grant me dis jolly harnaby of gongol:
Hell," he say, "is de crackling success
or smoking failure of a fire;
Heaven, a long walk up de tall Oliver.
Beyond dat you must find your own Tobillier exception.
You must do your own meditative mutter.
You must do your own shuttlecock adore."

* * *

Molecular dispersion. De best minds will agree to dat.
Perhaps you think that after death you wake up
on a conveyor belt with dirt, grass,
dead animals: "So this is where the dead go."
But if you believe in things at the chemical level,
de phlegm, sulfur, phlogiston dat make up a man
are borrowed after death by de plain work of microbes.
De glyptones and de anafracters go to work
and by de magic of de water table dey disperse
dese building blocks for de next assay,
fit subject for de next surmise.
Question is, "What happen to de spirit spark,
de *How am I feelin' today?* dat live
in de interstices of de body's interludes?"
Question is, "What happen to de wisp of awareness
dat make Ibn at de Go-to-Sleep
still Ibn in de 6 a.m.?" Question is,
"Is dis existence *To Be Continued,*
or is it time to roll de credits?"

One little theory or theorylette hold dat de long
oblong of de grave is not a place of cold and silence.
It a place of popcorn and comfort.
De inside of de lid is a movie screen.
De saved get to see first runs.
De lost must watch *Ishtar* for eternity.
(Bad karma? Dat's waking to find
you in de same coffin as Leroy Tisch.)
Have you heard of Puffer Netal, mortician of Grace?
Dey say he place thumbtacks, points-up, under the heads
of his subjects to hold dem heads-up in de coffin.
Dis make dem angry to de point of doom. Come
come-uppance day, dey going to stand in line to get at him.

Another theory hold dat like a sleight
de spirit never go in the box. Instead
upon the moment it slip into the nearest mirror
or varnished face of furniture or any shiny surface
and carry on its work, which is to reflect de world.
Shining of any kind add to de capacity.
When you wax a car you helpin' out. And over time
dis burden of spirits help to keep the world reflective.

Another hold dat you come back as what you most love.
Dis mean dat lovers of human kind come back as loved ones
(as to whether self-lovers get de best pay-off,
de theology don't get down dat far),
and lovers of dross—pelf, gold and the like—
go out of de story except as currency.

Another hold dat you come back as what you most deserve.
Under this regime the Prosecutor
come back as a dial tone; the Judge
he come back as a Nonaggression Pact.
Lady Overruth, she come back as a burgee
and Flavian, he come back as a bungee cord.
De Marquand come back as a house lice,
hangin' around de human follicles,
livin' by de bread of man alone,
waitin' to be magnified 800X.
Épergne, de Appreciator, come back as Bert Parks
singing "Here she come..." to Miss America.
Surcease, who give sadism a bad name,
he come back as a heart attack.
De prelate Combe come back as a Federal Fat Depository
and his assistant come to the party
dressed like a exit interview.

Another hold dat after death a man may return
on condition he live elsewhere on earth and not be recognized.
When I was in New York, each time a taxi driver
run repeatedly his gearshift through its H,
each time he share wid me the garlic of his night before,
I check to see if dat be Zoot Sebastepol.
He drive an armored personnel carrier
for de Marquand's personal use.
He hang from his rearview mirror not, you know,
de Playboy sign but a rag o' silk dat resemble
de bit-out crotch of a lady's underpants.
He live a violent life of de mind.
Small mammals he drive down for de fun
of being fell. He break for humans never.
Always he boogie to de other man's remorse.
A master of de infelicitous aside,
he was tagged for disposal when he was heard to say,
a few steps *shy* of out-of-earshot, "Stupid squeeze of shit.
Next time zip your lip so your brains don't fall out."

Today dey say dere is no Geode, Geode.
Dey say Opcit spend his day discoursing empty air;
dat I have *Quite...Rather...Much...*and *Did*
conversations wid myself. Dat's a creatal deal.
As if all de questions you be askin'
on a best-efforts basis to understand
the world weren't half de action in dis cell!
Serve dem right if I come back as you.
Now *dat* would be extravagant.
Imagine de correctitude of such an act.
It would be within de envelope of tricks
to go out like a brittle corpuscle,
and return from a stable of gossamer exquisites.

To go out like a special pleading,
and return like a triumph of spin control.
To go out like original sin,
and come back on a helluva note,
energized and potentized: a Zimbabwe express,
a Gallapagos *aussi* in a tangere *zeelee*.

But since de whimsy factor is on High,
if I was you I might return
widout your extra pieces of genetic stuff.
Trouble is, you leave light marks
on your environment. Wid you there's no show
on de meter of applause. I wouldn't sit there
like a whimsey picket in a cattle swoon.
I wouldn't wait like an alert novitiate.
If I was you I'd work my end
of de conversation somewhat harder.
Listen. Think. Find words. Reply.
Don't wait for earthquake to release the names.
I ask "How old are you?" What you mean, "Eleven fifteen"?
And I wouldn't snore. When you snore you sound like
you pronouncing *ichthyologist.*
Dat sudden intake over slacked aeolian
strings set de whole cell shuddering.
And you don't grind your teeth. You creak dem.
Not to mention how you chew. De purpose
is to bolus de food, to ready it for chyme.
When you sleep in the daytime your mouth, we note,
make a saliva slip, a silvery aside as if your tongue
fishing for wildlife in de cell. Cause de rest of us
to make book on what you going to catch.
If you would consider dese few amendments Ibn might not,
when he return, evolve from such a different compromise.

What I want to know, Geode, are we prematurely smug?
Brained the Spanish mackerel run the colors
of necrosis from iridesce to oily shale.
When his time come to take the seizure's turn,
will Ibn turn the colors of emancipation,
fluttering red then white then blue? Or will he,
sensing an unguinal deficiency, turn the color puce?
Will death to Ibn come as a muzzy embalm, musée interne,
quaternicus envalve, omphalos devoid?
Or does dying, dat slightly chaotic business of de soul,
give way like clear-air turbulence
to smooth approaches, happy landings?
Left Lane Ends, Geode, and so do we.
When comes dat call from de Land of Nod will Opcit,
like a prayer book in the wind,
open to all pages at once?

When Ibn go beneath the knife, may he use all
de solipsistic skills of his sophistic years.
When dey probe wid long slow scapular de inner ear's
dark archives of wax, when dey cause
de Eustachian tube to question its reason
for existence, may Ibn say "Dis not so bad,
Opcit's had of life of hard of hearing."
And of his teeth, when wid pliers dey remove
de metal consonants, may Ibn say
"'iss 'ot so bad." With denatured stumps
he will favor the soft foods favored by the old.
And when dey take his sight may he say
"Not so bad. Happened to Homer.
At least I won't be accused of *dis* again."
Piece by piece as de body fail may de spirit get to work.
When dey remove de long journeys in his legs,

may he say "Not so bad, dere will be less to wash,
less to work. And de rest of him is perfectly good."
And at de stilling of his kilted heart,
when dey take his brain, de final melon, may he say
"Dis not so bad, for Ibn love to sleep."

Will bits of Opcit rise in beak of puffin, belly of daw?
Or will he leave by long boat, as I believe.
In a roll of canvas, like a storm reef in a sail,
will he be committed to the deep, to join
de organic rain to deep pelagic feeders, de last chancers?
Where lobstermen farm de underside of de sea,
on a ground of coral sand, de assemblage dat was Opcit
peek from unsized, ill-sewn canvas: walnut knees,
shotput legs, de many-boned solutions of de feet—
like complicated metaphors for travel—
de arms like wings still folded in de canvas furrow,
de sly penis still looking for its chance, de medley of hands
wid dere sourcing ability, dere micro contemplations—
Oh, de diplomatic solutions of de hands,
which grow nails of horn only as an afterthought—
de fingers' pointed indicases, soft palps of indecision,
de head of ungrown hair, de Euphrates wafers of its ears,
de ribbed cage of de mouth, de set of de teeth
for saying's sake, de encompassed frenzy of de jaw:
all presided over by de visored helmet of de skull.
Tables turned, Opcit for once will play
host to de intemperate shrimp. Finally something
worth fighting over, an occasion for gratitude,
Opcit become his admirers. He find himself
on de feeding track of a benthic animal
which pause for a time, then move on.
Ashore, when Opcit's gone, let them carve for epiburg
this on his union stone: *Ohly Ohly In Free*

VI. THE WINGS OF MAN

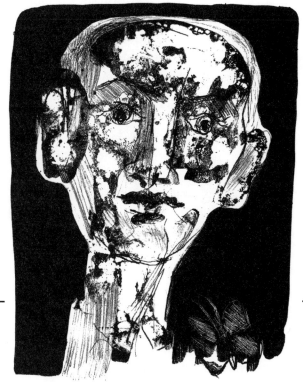

Lɪsᴛᴇɴ, Gᴇᴏᴅᴇ. Today Ibn begin.
With saved sisal he bend a sponson to a strut.
From rind of de coconut water call, bail
of a jailer's bucket, shards of an upset cup
he fashion a sprocket of burly intent.
By a treadle liberated from de sail shop
he introduce mechanical advantage.
From unroiled rattan, lath delivered of rude board bed,

he woof and warp a lie, even a place for Ibn's head.
From de slop dolly, de somewhat wobbly wicker stand
just the thing to get up speed. Strips of ticking
on a frame of necessary stress unfold.
The whole doped wid whatever: lye from the mortuary,
saliva slip collected from Geode's sleeping lip,
withheld pee, groinal efforts at reducing drag.
In de cell of his unmaking, a lumbar craft
take shape. Ibn ready to make his move.

It's a savory notion to wait until the hour
when dey walk de walls: Dey gas de cat.
Dey take de restraining clamps off the dogs;
dey inject them wid a note of optimism.
Or when the off-duty watch are at their mess
("I'll have de Whoremonger salad and Taskmaster steak,
medium well."). Perhaps Surcease havin' a padré soda,
and Sergeant Major, sittin' on de commode's cupped hand,
widout comment pass hard beans,
the aftermath of a jalapeño meltdown.
Perhaps de parapet guards, destabilized by wine,
in a wine slide, be distracted by a stopped train
where dey cleaning out some workers from de undertrucks.
Den Opcit, from de roof of dis empyrial hooskow,
make his mort sortie. Somewhat shy of octane
but ultralight from forced unfeeding,
from fasting on *ragout de pen* down
to de weight of no return, he take a running jump.
Across the prison yard his ungainly craft set sail.
To the greasy *Sombitch* of Surcease, the *For Heaven's Sake*
of the camp surgeon making a provisional cut,
over the heads of guards so breathtake
with *Goddamm* that they throw money after,

it flutter like flags of arrival, like a caper of *carpe diem*.
To the last words heard from him —
"You got to go along to get along." —
Opcit's craft *will* clear by inches the addle
of the outer wall (at this moment the Commandant,
Solange de Military North, his dripping dick in hand,
realize his myth quite far from his reality),
will reach the thermals rising from the sea's behest below.
As if an exact crouch will enable him to roost on air,
he will try the gulltrick: Either he will rodeo
convecting currents to a standmestill
or he will fall, in a probable plummet, most of a thousand feet
to rocks dat so far beat de sea, to take
a funny bounce, wid ghastly belches to expire.
To the tatter of antique rifles' imperfect fire,
the report of an AK-47 reading between the lines
of tracers that could be celebrating the craft
that draws such attention to its imperative,
he make an albatrossal fall.
He sail and sink at equal alarming rates.
Like a fiery trail of aftermath, like his own debris,
he follow the guidon of his own demise.
He drop like a dun aside into humidity's indistincts
where air and water more or less are one. He drop
like a gutshot angel to the sea's face far below,
to the waves that long preceded him,
that make a salad on his approach.

The suck and deep withdrawal of the fall,
by the vigorous pumping of his feet give way
to a moment of *OK*; with the swoop
of a fruit bat he pull up at the water's wait,
he hove to on the thin "between"

just shy of the Gulf's engulf.
He pedal and he steady up, he just maintain
his distance from the waves' own walk.
They gather in not-unfriendly fashion beneath his feet,
white-faced they make a green accord
which Ibn touches never quite.
Maintaining inches of altitude
(no danger of Daedalean overreach
let alone de overreach of Overruth),
on the lip of failure he abide.
By the quiet creak of wicker's work
he observe a fragile truce with gravity,
a sacrament that holds.

In the success of a fall not fallen into
he ride on a purity of intent, he dory on consequence.
Opcit's quadriceps, the huff of Ibn's leather lungs
fuel his Make-fly on a weight of words.
He hexameter the waves, he chanty an uncorrupted air.
Cautious of wave's cuff, the catch of a caught strut,
he remains scatheless in this matter of pedaling the ocean's face.
He gains his stride like a heyday, as if perpetual motion
something he might put his money in. Hinding the wind,
the ornithopter with its barefoot burden
banks lightly above the Come-by-Lovely Banks
(the gradual of ground appearing from the deep,
the aqua gathering of shoals, the detail of fishes).
He avoids horizon held by the line of easy landfall,
of clouds by Claudel. He cardinals the compass,
by a deep memory heads sou' by sou' sou'.
He finds beauty in twilight's loss of certainty.
The moon, bearing the Sea of Tranquility,
rises as if bespoken in his name.

And it may be the histories will aver:
when dawn was no more than a bevel of light,
there was a low heraldry of land,
even a *get* of runway lights, the blue for the red.
And he will land. And they will come out from their noshes,
wiping their mouths, and say *Do you swear?*
And he will say *We shall see.*

ABOUT THE AUTHOR

John Barr has pursued parallel careers as poet and investment banker
for the past twenty-five years. He has founded the country's largest
natural gas marketing company and a prominent investment-banking
boutique. He is President Emeritus of the Poetry Society of America,
and Chairman of the Board of Bennington College. Story Line Press
published the trade edition of his first book, *THE HUNDRED FATHOM
CURVE*, in 1997. He lives with his wife and three children in Westchester
County, New York.